River's Shadow

River's Shadow

Timothy Went

PALMETTO
PUBLISHING
Charleston, SC
www.PalmettoPublishing.com

Copyright © 2024 by Timothy Went

All rights reserved
No portion of this book may be reproduced, stored in a retrieval system, or transmitted in any form by any means–electronic, mechanical, photocopy, recording, or other–except for brief quotations in printed reviews, without prior permission of the author.
Paperback ISBN: 9798822967380

Chapter 1

Fog thick & heavy, it just rained in the forest. River runs. A deep sense of dread pushing down on her. She tries to remember how she got here. The last thing she remembers is getting ready for bed with Jenna. They were talking about something at work, she tries to remember the details & is pulled from her thoughts as she runs into a wet branch, drenching herself even more. She keeps running, all she remembers is the two of them laughing, hugging & kissing each other goodnight. The deep sense of dread returns, River hears branches breaking, and a bird squawking. Despite the running & sweating, she feels chills all the way to her bones. Her legs burning, her side acheing, she keeps running, looking for anything to help her, a road, a house, even a campfire. But she sees nothing but fog, some trees, & the brush. She smells the forest, it's wet from the rain, but there's something else, something putrid that makes her stomach churn. River pushes hard, when she stumbles she crawls & scrambles to a tree trying to pull herself up, the bark of the tree slick from the rain. River turns her back to it the kool bark cooling her skin through her shirt, she runs her fingers through drenched black hair, chest heaving as she struggles to catch her breath. As River's heart pounds in her chest & ears movement catches her eye, and her breath catches in her throat as a small black cat jumps onto a stump. It sits there looking at her, a slightly amused look on its face. Ears pointing outward eyes slightly squinted. As River focuses on the cat's eyes she sees they are black orbs in its sockets so black the light just seems drawn in. Then she notices stripes in the cat's fur, swirling as she focuses on the stripes she can't tell if they are white or silver. River does notice, as impossible as it seems the cat is dry. Then she hears a thought in her head, not a voice but a thought, it sounds like her own words, what are you doing sitting against that tree? River is uncertain what is happening. The black cat just keeps watching her still looking amused. Another thought enters River's mind, sounding like her inner voice again, why do you look afraid it asks. Do you not know me? River feels panic & fear grip her as she feels the presence again, whatever was chasing her is close again. River jumps to her feet ignoring the small black cat, she spins her head searching. She hears her inner thoughts again, River turn & face your fear. River's heart catches in her throat, feeling pure terror, she turns slowly, to see a dark shadow peering around the tree at her. Slowly its head raises, River's breath catches in her burning lungs, as the shadow creature's head raises she sees human-looking eyes, slightly larger than normal, a slight recognition as she realizes they are similar to her own. But the shadow creature's eyes are just dark voids, hers she realizes with some relief are jade green, her relief is short-lived as the shadow keeps raising its head she sees all similarities end, its mouth opening wide she sees tentacles where its lips should be. The shadow opens its mouth wide, River feels a pull on her, unlike anything she felt before. A new level of fear grips her as she begins to realize it's pulling on her very essence, her soul. River's eyes fill with tears, shes about to die & she knows it, thoughts of Jenna race through her mind, the first time they met, the first time they held hands, & the first kiss. Her lips tremble as she remembers telling Jenna she loves her for the first time, the way Jenna's blue eyes lit up & her little smile crossed her beautiful face, as Jenna leaned her head forward, blushing long blonde hair falling over her eyes. Shell never forgot Jenna's reply as Jenna said, you better River I love you too. River feels her heartbeat slow, either from death being so close or from the realization that she will never hold Jenna again, River's tears come as she thinks of her aunt Bella, it has only been six months since they buried River's parents, six months since Aunt Bella lost her sister. Aunt Bella never knew River before that day. River's parents adopted her from an orphanage at the age of two, & lived in another state, her dad working for a city engineering company couldn't leave his job, she never knew what her mom did, all she knows as shes facing death is she never really knew them. Before her thoughts can continue, she hears her inner voice again, River says, why are you afraid of shadows? They are your playthings remember? That's when River realizes, that her inner thoughts since she saw the cat may sound like her voice but it is the cat speaking to her. Then she hears, River, you should just wake up now, it will be easier. River thinks to herself, wake up now? Again the last memories she had before running in the forest flood in, laughing with Jenna before bed, hugging & kissing her, & saying I love you.

Chapter 2

River jolts awake, sweating, shivering, & panting. Her heart rages inside her chest, she looks around, disoriented and confused. The darkness was broken only by the light of the alarm clock. Jenna stirs, partially awake asking River if she is okay. River takes her hand pulls her close kissing her deeply lips trembling, then tells Jenna how much she loves her. Jenna worried even more now asks her, what's wrong River? River keeps her head against Jenna's taking a deep breath and letting it out in a sigh, and tells Jenna about her nightmare. Jenna holds River close with her head on her breast, stroking her hair. Jenna tells her it's okay now I've got you, my love, it was just a nightmare. River lays there taking in Jenna's scent, as Jenna dozes off River reflects on her nightmare, still feeling all the fear & dread. Wondering about the things the cat said, especially "River why are you afraid of shadows? They are your playthings remember? " River trembles with a shiver, even with Jenna's body close to hers, the cat had also asked if River remembered it. As River finally settles into sleep she decides to try and find out more about her past, hopefully her aunt Bella knows how to help her.

That night River sleeps through her alarm, Jenna wakes up and reaches over and shuts off the alarm. Jenna watches her love sleeping, smiling to herself thinking about how much she loves her. Jenna can't help herself, remembering how she met River, it was raining as it tends to in Oregon, Jenna was sitting in her grandmother's gazebo in her backyard, missing her parents, still wondering why they divorced. Moving away was their choice, not hers. Since she was fifteen at the time she was given the choice of which parent to live with, she didn't want to leave her small town, and definitely not her grandmother, so even with breaking hearts she chose her grandmother. Her parents of coarse didn't like that and haven't spoken to her since. So when Jenna isn't at school or work she spends time with her grandmother, with lectures about spending time with kids her age and things like going outside and playing. But Jenna knows her grandmother does it with love. The day she met River, her grandmother was out, probably playing bingo, or whatever she does with her spare time, Jenna just studies or works when she's out. That day though she chose to sit in the gazebo & watch it rain. Her neighbor Bella, a nice lady had been out of town, she didn't know why, and was returning. She watched her car come down the road seeing someone in the passenger seat. The person was small, head down with a hood over it, Jenna was curious because in all the time she'd had known Bella, Jenna hadn't seen her bring anyone home. So she pulled the hood of her sweater up over her blonde hair and went to say hello. When she got to the car Bella smiled at her and got out, hugged Jenna as she usually did when seeing her. Bella said hello to her and said I want to introduce you to my niece

Jenna. Now Jenna was extremely curious, in all the years she'd known Bella she didn't know she had a family. Of course, Jenna said absolutely Bella. When the girl got out of the car though she walked right past them to Bella's front door, Jenna looked at Bella confused, Bella smiled politely & said don't be offended Jenna, River is shy, she was, & Bella hesitated a bit, then said born with a small birth defect, and to make things worse we just came from her parents funeral. Shocked Jenna quietly asked, both parents? Bella sniffled & said yes Jenna. Jenna didn't know what to say, Bella just said Jenna, you go wait by the door with River, I'll get my bags & be there in a moment. Jenna hesitated but seeing Bella wasn't taking no for an answer finally said okay. Walking up to the door Jenna was nervous, she didn't know what to say to River, or if she'd even let Jenna talk to her. When Jenna got there she did the only thing she could think of & being raised in a small town like Wheeler Oregon, this was how it was done. So she stepped up to River, & said hello River I'm Jenna, I'm sorry for your loss & held her arms out to hug her letting River decide. Jenna was nervous, then surprised as River stepped into her & hugged her tight, after a moment River looked up at her, and Jenna saw the biggest jade green eyes she'd ever seen, realizing this must be the birth defect Bella spoke of Jenna could only think of one thing to say, I love jade she said especially green, Rivers smile was all Jenna needed. After coming back from her memory Jenna leaned forward & gently kissed River's lips & whispered to her, sleep my love I'll be right back. Jenna took a shower, dried off & wrapped herself in a towel grabbed her toothbrush & went back out into the bedroom to wake River. When Jenna stepped up next to the bed, River started to wake up on her own, big jade eyes blinking at Jenna. Jenna pulled the toothbrush from her mouth & said good morning sleepy head. River stretched & yawned, rubbing sleep from her eyes, and asked what time it was. Jenna said seven-thirty. So if you're going to work tonight you need to get ready. River stretched got up hugged & kissed Jenna, Jenna asked if she was okay & what she wanted to do. River said I'll shower & get ready for work, then leaned back a little, smiling she asked Jenna if she'd like to join her. Jenna smiled back & said you slept in love, you shower & I'll go make breakfast. River sighed, kissed her & said okay your right see you downstairs. Walking to the bathroom River thought to herself, & bout her dream. Not really wanting to be alone but Jenna was right. As she stepped into the shower she thought about what the cat had asked, don't you remember me? Suddenly her mind was swimming, a long-lost memory started to form. She heard a little girl's laughter & seen a big room, in what looked like a very old building. Unfortunately, nothing more came to her, so she decided to speak to her aunt about her parents, & the dream.

Chapter 3

River checks herself in the mirror. Large jade green eyes stare back at her, she vividly flashes back to the hunter in her dream. Panic rises again, just as intense as it was in the dream. River closes her eyes. Breathes deeply, hands like vices on the sink, body trembling. When she opens her eyes again it's just her reflected in the mirror. She moves from the bathroom and quickly gets dressed, even more determined to find answers, she heads downstairs to talk to her aunt.

River rushes downstairs, feeling the anticipation & nervousness about what's to come. As she enters the kitchen she sees Jenna setting the table, River notices a plate on the table, it has a tuna fish sandwich on it. If she were to guess Jenna made it trying to cheer her up after her nightmare, her mouth waters some as she begins to crave the sandwich, thinking of the mustard & paprika. River refocuses noting the glass of black tea another favorite of hers, Jenna is definitely trying to help her feel better. As she moves to her chair she is glad to see her aunt sitting at the table, some nights her aunt is too tired to join them. However after a quick smile & whispered thank you to Jenna she noticed her aunt, sitting forward arms on the table, Bella looking expectant & also a little sad. River not sure what to think of this takes a bite of her sandwich. Definitely one of Jenna's best tuna fish sandwiches. After swallowing her bite she looks at her aunt Bella already nervous about what's to come, she wipes her sweaty palms on her pants, then says, Aunt Bella, I need to talk to you before I leave tonight. Her aunt Bella just nods & says I'm here for you River. Seeing her aunt isn't surprised & is already supportive makes her curious, she glances sideways at Jenna, Jenna looks nervous & extremely focused on her own meal. With a sigh River begins by explaining her dream, as she recounts what happened she's there again, as if it's happening right now. Her voice becomes fearful, she's panting short of breath. Sweating as though she's running again. River explains the black cat, telling how it spoke into her mind chilled as she explains, it was with my own voice. Then taking a deep breath she looks into her aunt's eyes, aunt Bella, why would the black cat ask me why I don't remember it? Bella takes a moment & then says River tell me the rest, what else happened in your dream? River thinks about this for a moment, taking Jenna's hand she realizes her aunt doesn't seem surprised, just concerned. Curious about her aunt & a little suspicious she continues. River says there was a shadow chasing me, River feels the sense of dread again fear grasping her heart. River squeezes Jenna's hand feeling safe & secure with her love. She describes the shadow, fighting the fear growing stronger inside her. She says I looked in its eyes, they looked like my own, except instead of jade they were just black holes in its sockets. Then she describes its mouth, as just a giant open maw with tentacles, but it felt like it was sucking my soul from me pulling my essence from me. As she finishes River downs half her glass of tea, taking a deep breath she looks at her aunt. Bella doesn't look surprised, but she looks afraid, her skin white her hands in front of her, fingers clasped together, knuckles white. River watches her aunt, seeing the lack of surprise & the fear she asks, Jenna did you tell Aunt Bella about my dream? Jenna said no, when I came downstairs to start breakfast Aunt Bella was already there. We said hello & aunt Bella said stay close, River will need you. Even more suspicious River looks her aunt Bella in the eye & says I have to know. Bella takes a moment, says River eat your breakfast, please. River eats waiting. Finally, after what seems like forever Bella says, I can't show you what you're not ready to see, I can't teach you what you're not ready to learn, however, I caution you, the hunter is coming & only you can stop him if anyone can. River looks at Bella, & asks the hunter? Bella says the shadow from your dream, River says that is just a dream, that cathululips thing can't hurt me, it's not real is it? After her aunt just looks at her for a moment, Jenna says, it's not real River, just a nightmare. River eyes her aunt, and says more, you know more tell me, please. Swallowing hard Bella says, your mother had a secret, but she's gone now, & I'm not certain of what she did but I know before you were born, after college she disappeared. I didn't hear from her until you were born, & even then she just sent the picture of her holding you. River tears up a little, she knows the picture, Bella gave it to her at her parent's funeral, the only picture she has of her mother, she never got one of her father. Jenna still holding river's hand says, aunt Bella there's more please tell us. Bella looks sad, tears in her eyes, & with a sniffle says, Shadow

Haven Orphanage. Bella continues, I'm sorry you two I really don't know more, but if there are answers they are there. River looks at Jenna a moment, Jenna says, in the morning River let's go to the library, we can find out more. River nods & looks at her aunt & asks, what does an orphanage have to do with this? Bella is quiet for a moment then says, when your mother disappeared after college I hired a private investigator to find her, the police didn't look long. The investigator said he'd tracked her there, this is why I caution you, I haven't heard from him since. Both River & Jenna take a deep breath, looking at each other they are both nervous & unsettled. Bella says you to need to get to work, love you both, Bella sniffles & through tears says I'll clean up dinner & see you both tomorrow. River & Jenna heard the sadness & hope in Bella's voice as she said that. River & Jenna get up from the table walk over & hug Bella, they tell her they love her & leave for work. While Bella is sitting there she lights a cigarette, drawing the smoke in as she thinks she may have just lost the rest of her family, & what's left of her sister. That's when a small black cat jumps up in her lap, looking up into her eyes, silver white swirls in its fur.

River & Jenna head out the door on the way Jenna grabs their lunch, not really feeling it, River asks what's for lunch? Jenna smiles & says something you'll like, River smiles slightly & says thank you love. When they get in the car they both sigh, neither of them excited to go to work after talking to their aunt. River's mind is racing as she starts the car & barely checks her mirrors before pulling out of the driveway. Jenna's mind is racing too, for the first time in her life of knowing Bella & definitely for the first time since she started calling her aunt, Jenna feels she was not entirely honest. Finally, Jenna can't stand it anymore, reaching over she puts her hand on River's thigh, when River looks over at her she smiles but seeing it's more than just making physical contact she asks Jenna what is it? Jenna thinks of the best way she can to talk about this, finally, she just asks are we gonna talk about this. River looks ahead, sighs & lays her hand on top of Jenna's giving it a squeeze & says we better. Jenna taking that as her opening starts out with River I'm sorry but I gotta ask, do you also think Aunt Bella lied? River already thinking of all this says, I'm not sure she lied but I'm sure she didn't tell us everything. She didn't even try talking about the black cat. Jenna says, you're right, all she seemed to care about was the shadow chasing you. River says she named it, remember she said "Tell me about the hunter". They both fall silent looking at each other. Both a little afraid. River starts to think of a way to explain to Jenna she may need to leave her afraid the hunter may hurt her or worse, & that's when River's eyes tear up. When she sniffles Jenna looks back at her seeing the tears, immediately Jenna asks River what's wrong. River parking the car outside the hotel just looks at Jenna, not sure how to say it. Jenna sees what's happening & leans in hugging River, leans back looking her in the eyes & says, River I'm not leaving you, not even for my own safety, she looks at her a bit longer a very serious look on her face. Finally, River lets out the breath she was holding & whispers ok ok Jenna. Jenna kisses her softly, when she's done River looks at her & says I'm sorry Jenna I had to at least think about it. Jenna does her best to smile sweetly despite the situation & says, I know River it's because you love me. River nods reaching up & running the fingers of one hand through Jenna's bangs over her ear & says let's get through tonight. The girls go to work & straight to the basement, thankfully before Jenna's grandmother passed she was able to call her old friend who runs the hotel & get them jobs here, late at night in the laundry room basement River doesn't have to worry people will stare at her. Jenna can work & attend school this way as well, though thanks to River's help she graduated just after she turned sixteen. Going into the laundry room the girls see four of the six washers full & only one load in one of the six dryers, River sighs & says it figures they left would wash the sheets & leave us to dry them. Jenna trying to be cheerful says, job security. Chuckling River says at least we'll be busy sooner. The two get started, making small talk & discussing going to the library after work to learn about Shadow Haven. River asks Jenna what she thinks they'll find? Jenna trying to make light of it says, a beautiful orphanage where all the children live beautiful lives. They both laugh, & River says with a name like Shadow Haven how could it be anything else? The two get the sheets out of the dryer & fold them, deciding to take lunch before they take them upstairs to the linen closet. As they sit down for lunch Jenna snatches the bag from River that has their lunches, River just looks at her amused look on her face, Jenna looks up at her shyly & says something special remember? River smiles, through the night & their joking she's forgotten her worries for the moment, not to mention River is a sucker for Jenna's smile. Jenna makes a show of rooting through their lunch bag purposely taking out her lunch first, River laughs echoing through the employee lounge says, I'm going to starve here, anticipation won't fill me up. Jenna chuckles & says fine miss impatient, smiling brightly proud of herself Jenna pulls out a very thick tuna sandwich placing it on the paper plate in front of River followed by a small bottle of black tea. River seeing this smiles & looks up at Jenna, the two share a long loving look. Jenna finally says eat your lunch tell me what you think, it's not just a big tuna sandwich there's more. River being curious pulls away the seran-wrap instantly she smells mustard & something else, not sure what it is but trusting Jenna she picks up the tuna stuffed bread & takes a bite, her eyes widen as she chews. Jenna watching with a smile on her face, enjoying her reaction. Jenna waits for her to swallow & says I think I got you spoiled now. They chuckle a moment & River says, only you do my love thank you & thank you for the jalapeno mustard. Jenna smiles proud of herself & not saying a word starts eating her own sandwich. After lunch, the girls go back downstairs grabbing their cart full of folded sheets & go to the elevator to head to their first & maybe only stop, the third-floor linen closet. Jenna makes small talk on the way, wondering out loud if the linen closet will be full or not. When they get there River feels a cold chill, she hesitates a moment with her key to the closet, Jenna watches her from behind the cart. After just a moment the chill passes & River brushes it off & unlocks the door. Once open the girls are overwhelmed by a putrid smell. Jenna gags & asks what is that? Did something die in there? River knowing exactly what that smell is immediately turns around & rushes past the cart to grab Jenna's arm saying we gotta run now! Jenna confused forgetting that part of River's description of her dream hesitates & asks why? Before River can stop her Jenna looks around the cart into the linen closet. Jenna's eyes widen, and her mouth hangs open paralyzed with fear. River seeing what Jenna sees in the doorway yanks Jenna after her. River gets Jenna running thankfully River is thinking & heads to the stairwell around the corner knowing if they have to wait for the elevator it's over. River & Jenna run downstairs & find the boiler room run inside they head to the back behind the boiler. With nowhere else to run they stop & look at each other, both react at the same moment & hold each other crying softly. Jenna between sobbs whispers to River, that was the cathululips thing! It's real! the Shadow Hunter is what Aunt Bella called it right? River feeling her panic & fear notices something different this time, there's no dread. Sure she's afraid & panicked but the dread of it devouring her soul isn't present. As she thinks about this she whispers in Jenna's ear, yes that's cathululips from my dream, hold me tight Jenna it's going to be ok. Jenna listens to River, not sure how it's going to be ok or how River knows it will be but she trusts & loves her so she tries to calm herself. While River & Jenna were running away the Shadow Hunter stepped out into the hall to pursue them as it turned to its right passing the elevator a small black cat steps out behind the girls from inside the closest guest room. The Shadow Hunter sees the small black cat thinking nothing of it. As the small black cat walks out into the hall from the recessed guest room doorway it looks up at the Shadow Hunter & speaks one command into its mind, halt! The Shadow Hunter confused stops unknowingly obeying the small black cat's command. The small black cat's ears turn on its head listening as River & Jenna run downstairs, the small black cat returns its full focus back to the Shadow Hunter and then sits down its tail begins to flick playfully & it narrows its eyes laying it's ears to the sides completely amused. The Shadow Hunter not being amused becomes enraged again taking a step forward the Shadow Hunter hears the small black cat's voice in its head again. Calmly the small black cat says, you too seem to have forgotten me.

The Shadow Hunter hesitates, it fully understands the black cat but what it doesn't understand is that the small black cat expects it to remember it & it doesn't understand why it sounds just like its prey. The small black cat speaks again, leave this place Hunter, she is not ready for you. The Shadow Hunter returns to its rage it doesn't know what this cat really is but the Hunter doesn't know fear, so it steps forward again. The small black cat doesn't change its amused stance at all, nor its tone of voice as it speaks into the Hunter's mind again. I will only warn you once more Hunter leave, you are no concern of mine I only care for the girl, if you want to test me you better meet me at low noon, then the shadows will fall. Hearing this for the first time in its existence the Shadow Hunter feels fear & confusion. Between the two emotions the Shadow Hunter even if it doesn't understand why heeds the small black cat's warning, returning to the shadows. The small black cat content with the outcome of this situation makes its way to the hotel kitchen to find itself a meal. After the confrontation between the small black cat & the Shadow Hunter ends River feels the change happening around her, and her fear & panic evaporate. Taking a deep breath she turns her attention to Jenna holding her face between her hands & looking her in the eyes, she tells Jenna it's ok now the Hunter is gone. Jenna looks confused before she can ask River kisses her gently then takes her by the hand & says let's go finish up if you're still committed my love we better go to the library right after work. Jenna hearing this feels calmer, her trust in River giving her strength she moves up beside River holding her hand & says I'm with you River from now till always.

Chapter 4

Bella looks down exhaling cigarette smoke from her nose as the small black cat jumps onto her lap, as she reaches down to pet him he begins kneading her skirt getting comfortable, and purring slightly. Bella takes another drag of her cigarette, as she exhales she says hello Odiewan, I expected you sooner. The small black cat curled in a ball in Bella's lap says to her, I was occupied my apologies, Bella. As Bella continues to smoke she says it's OK my old friend I understand. They sit in silence for a minute Bella smoking & petting Odiewan. After Bella puts out her cigarette she asks Odiewan, how bad is it this time? Odiewan is quiet for a bit just enjoying the company of his old friend, finally, he says, bad enough to require a human shadow hybrid & a knight of the Oracle. Bella sighs nervous & worried thinking about the two girls, then she realizes what Odiewan had said & asks, a knight of the Oracle? Odiewan chuckles & says, time has taken a toll on you my old friend, I refer to the golden-haired child, the knight devoted to the Shadow Girl. Bella realizing whom he's speaking of sighs & says you are correct Odiewan I have fallen out of practice over time, I had no idea Jenna was a knight. Odiewan purring contently says, you couldn't have known she doesn't know either for the time of her knighting has not arrived. As Bella lights another cigarette she asks, should I even ask how you know? Odiewan is quiet for a bit & when he replies simply says, how I know isn't what is important, the fact that I know is, more importantly, what the golden-haired girl does with it once she knows is the most important. Bella considers this as she smokes, she expects riddles from Odiewan knowing he answered her question completely leaving it to her to decipher the true meaning. Then she tears up remembering what she can recall of the knights, & whispers oh no Odiewan. Odiewan continues to purr in her lap, not saddened or concerned about Bella's epiphany. Finally, Bella asks Odiewan, they are going to make it tonight right? I know the Shadow Hunter hunts tonight. Odiewan responds with another riddle, no fates are sealed, no futures told, save for the strength of the Shadow Girl & the undying devotion of the Knight. Bella chuckles to herself enjoying her cigarette, of course, he'd us a riddle, and then she fully understands what Odiewan said, through tears of happiness she pets her old friend & says thank you. Odiewan lays in Bella's lap for a time enjoying his old friend's company, then raises his head becoming alert to something. Bella asks if he's ok, Odiewan turns in her lap, raises up puts his front legs on her chest, and looks Bella in the eyes. Bella notes he looks sad, ears drooping & his eyes half-lidded as he looks at her. Odiewan nuzzles her & says, tell the Shadow Girl more she's not prepared enough, then looking her in the eyes again says something Bella has never heard from him before. Goodbye, old friend. Then without another word Odiewan jumps from her lap & runs from the kitchen.

Chapter 5

The rest of the night was good for River & Jenna. They finally were able to calm down focusing on their work & discussing what happened & what to do. River says I think two things Jenna, one we go see Aunt Bella before we go to the library, & two Jenna, & River looks her in the eyes, firmly & confidently says, we run no more. Jenna surprised thinks about this, then asks no more running? River sighs & says I'm not sure how Jenna but we must fight back, running seems to only be drawing this out. Remember what the little black cat asked me? Jenna thinks about that for a minute & says about shadows being your play things, Do you really think there's a connection? River says, I don't know for certain but remember Aunt Bella called it a Shadow Hunter & with what the cat said, well just maybe it all means something. Jenna & River talk about this slowly putting together what they have learned & agreeing with all the impossible that's happening maybe just maybe it's possible River can stand up to the Shadow Hunter. After work, they go straight to Aunt Bella not knowing if they'll get answers or more questions. When the girls get home they are surprised to see Aunt Bella asleep on the couch, on the floor an ashtray, next to it, her cigarettes & lighter. The two look at each other knowing Bella as they do, they know she must have gone to sleep worried or upset. They go to the kitchen, they make coffee & breakfast for Bella & decide to shower & change before talking to her. Once in the shower River & Jenna face each other, searching each other for answers & strength. They both wrap their arms around each other, River whispers into Jenna's ear, I love you from now until forever Jenna. Jenna hears her words and feels her love, smiling to herself she begins to feel more confident, for a moment she hears her grandmother's voice in her head as though she's right beside her, I'm happy you finally found someone Jenna, keep River close to you she will always fill your heart. Jenna wonders why this memory feeling as though it's happening now is so vivid, she can feel her grandmother's hand holding hers as the same as it happened when her grandmother had first done this. She doesn't have time to think on this long though as she feels River turn her around & begin brushing her blonde hair. After the girls are done getting dressed they head downstairs to find their aunt sitting at the table, a sad smile on her face she says good morning you two & thank you for making breakfast. The girls look at each other and then giggle, they both don't see it as a surprise their aunt beat them to breakfast. Sipping her coffee Bella motions for them to sit, once they do Bella sets her coffee down & says alright girls it's time to talk. Both of the girls just wait in anticipation, not sure what to expect.

In another realm.... confused & afraid the Shadow Hunter stands upright, even for him traversing the portals between realms hurts. Especially this time driven by his fear of the small black cat he didn't take any time to check his location, only that the destination was correct. As he shakely brings himself to his feet he doesn't take time to look behind him, as he leans back his right foot moves back to correct his balance finding nothing. He falls from the ledge he was on, as he falls anger grows as he realizes he did this to himself. He lets out a roar of rage before he finally impacts what passes for the ground here, black semi-hardened sludge. He lays there a moment this time taking a moment to collect himself. As he sits up he looks around, all he sees is the dark sky broken by the landscape, black & mostly formless. He brings himself to his feet reaching with his mind to feel his destination. With no sun or moon not even stars there's no other way, not even landmarks. He feels the Unseen One's presence, thankfully he's close. He begins walking in the direction he needs to go, thinking to himself about how he's failed & what may happen to him. It's all that small black cat's fault, not a cat he knows this is something far more powerful he thinks back to what he felt in his mind. The small black cat used the female's voice to speak to him, even more so its power, he shivers remembering, it was more powerful than The Unseen Ones. This gives the Hunter hope, once he explains his failure forgiveness will be granted, and he moves forward determination restored. Returning here brings back the memories of his first time here. He was young, how young he does not know as he doesn't even know his age. He'd just killed over 200 humans didn't even know what they were called at the time, after he just stood over his last kill, he'd devoured this ones soul still feeling the rush of the fear & dread of his prey, that's when it happened a portal opened directly under him when it was over he was here, the neither realm he was told. The Unseen Ones spoke into his mind powerful & painfully, they said they'd summoned him feeling his power & strength, but they were displeased. They did not expect a hybrid nor a child for this they had cast him out. He was lost & alone, & for years he fought shadow things & other abominations to survive. Then one day it happened & he still doesn't know why, another portal opened again & just like before directly underneath him & he fell. This time stronger, older, & he knew what was happening & so he landed on his feet ready but for what, he didn't know. The Unseen Ones roared into his head, kneel! The hunter kneeled immediately, fear & panic forcing his obedience. The Unseen Ones were quick to tell him what they wanted & expected. Nullsoul is the name in which you will be granted, we have a proposal for you. He was frightened & confused they had cast him out years ago & even if he'd only learned loneliness & survival he was smart enough to know if creatures this powerful wanted him for anything it was probably going to be something he'd better take very seriously. The Unseen One's voices penetrated him to his core as he listened, you have been chosen for a task you, are to travel to the realm of your creation, there you will hunt a Shadow Girl for one purpose & one purpose only devour her soul. He was confused but also tempted, from what he could remember of his realm it was far better than where he'd been & from what he could tell better than this realm as well. The Unseen Ones spoke again interrupting his thoughts, if you succeed you will be rewarded & you can join this realm as a servant to us, you will be granted many things that you can't imagine. They go silent, perhaps giving him a moment to think, & he does for just a moment & he knows this is something, a chance he'd better take. That was all the time he had to think before they spoke again, this time a warning for if he failed. Failing us will result in punishment unending, & immediately he felt pain, so much pain all he could do is collapse & spasm. Focus Nullsoul he tells himself pulling himself from that memory. He sees the opening in the ground to where he must go to communicate with The Unseen Ones, looking at it still disgusts even him, dripping, pulsating, it's repulsive but he supposes that's by design to keep others away. He enters, walking down into the darkness, the ground soft & mushy under his feet. As he walks he looks around knowing that the unending punishment they spoke of could mean any of the things he's seeing here in the darkness. Creatures being tortured in various ways, some skinned alive not being allowed to die, others having their bodies violated in ways he doesn't understand. Some being beaten, burned, & drowned. He walks on, the tortured souls here mean nothing to him. His fear of his failure is all he's concerned with. As he enters the void he steps forward immediately he's in unbearable pain, collapsing to the floor, The Unseen Ones already know! As he spasms in pain on the floor he hears their voice, Nullsoul you were warned of what would happen if you failed us! Nullsoul forces himself to speak desperation being just strong enough to force out these words, let...me...explain...before....judgment he gasps. For a moment the pain continues he thinks they may not listen, then he feels intense pain inside his head, & the memories of going into the realm of the Shadow Girl flood into perspective & the small black cat, that memory he sees twice. He thinks to himself that's good! See why I failed then perhaps ull forgive me. The pain does stop, though he decides not to stand, showing he's still loyal he just gets to his knees & waits. After what seems like forever The Unseen Ones finally speak, Nullsoul you may have failed however in your failure you have brought us information, information just important enough to save yourself this time. This time he thinks, then I mustn't fail again. They speak to him again, your mission will change for a time, succeed in this mission, prove your loyalty & we will grant you what you will need to kill the Shadow Girl. Nullsoul says of course it will be done, but what of that small black cat? Immediately in pain, he collapses & starts spasming again. Do not question us! Do as you are told! The pain stops & again he takes a knee & says it will be done please give me my targets scent. When the Unseen Ones give him the scent he flinches unsure why, however, he knows he cannot fail again.

Chapter 6

As the girls sit there looking at Bella expectantly, Bella chuckles & says you two can eat while I talk it's not likely your going to sleep today. River & Jenna look at each other & smile sheepishly, they know Bella's right, so they begin eating. Bella takes a moment not sure where to start, after thinking about it she takes a deep breath & says, I don't have all of your answers girls, for this I am truly sorry. She hesitates a moment watching the girls, she wonders who's more nervous, thinking about having a cigarette she decides to wait until they finish eating. Bella continues, there's been a war going on since the beginning of this realm, it has managed not to fall to its enemies but at some point it will fall unless the portal or portals can be sealed again. Bella pauses watching the girls, she's happy to see that so far at least they are taking this well, she says no, I do not know how many portals are open but there is at least one. She waits and watches as the girls take this information in, again they seem to be doing well. Bella continues, there are forces for both sides mind you, she hesitates & finally finds the courage to say, I am one of the forces fighting for this realm, I am a Valkyrie. Bella doesn't wait for their reaction this time she just continues, most of what you may have heard of my kind is not true, the myths, folklore, they have it wrong. Now she pauses, seeing they have finished eating she reaches for her cigarettes & lighter, lighting her cigarette she takes a long drag, holding it in. River listening to what she's saying realizes something, after Bella lights her cigarette River gently takes the lighter from Bella's hand & holds it between herself & Jenna. As Bella exhales she says, that's the symbol of my people, sword only as we believe a shield shows weakness. Jenna looks at Bella & says, never have I thought you were weak Aunt Bella, River says me neither, in fact, aunt Bella with your help & guidance I'm here with you & Jenna now. Bella smiled softly tearing up, & says thank you girls. Now let me go on, she takes another drag of her cigarette, contemplating what to say next. Finally, she says, for 45 years I have done what I can to defend this realm even sacrificing my sister. That makes both girls sit up straight paying closer attention then before. Bella continues, yes it's true River your mother went away to college & we didn't speak after that, but it's what happened before that & before you were born that is important for you to know. Bella pauses as she puts her cigarette out letting her last drag slowly out from her nose. River & Jenna holding hands, both intensely focused. Finally, Bella continues, we were part of a society called the Watchers of Shadow. Basically, we made sure that the portal we were tasked with watching could not be opened. Your mother River was born human as I told you I am not, for years she hid her jealousy from me, but our parents & myself knew it was there. Bella tears up again a little, sniffles & continues. When your mother left for college we knew from the fact that she didn't tell us everything about what she was studying to be suspicious, but we couldn't imagine how disastrous it would be. River & Jenna watch her listening, River thinking if this is going at all like I think it is my mother must have done something terrible, aunt Bella is here, not apart of some group or society, Jenna has lived next to her her whole life. Then River takes a deep breath reminding herself she hasn't heard everything yet, so she realizes she must be patient. Bella lights another cigarette & then continues, while your mother was at college I was given orders to move here, living next to your grandmother Jenna, Bella remembering her conversation with Odiewan & putting it all together she laughs out loud. The girls watch confused, finally, River whispers to Jenna that may not be a cigarette she's smoking, not being able to help themselves the girls begin to giggle. After it all stops Bella says I assure you it's just a cigarette girls, but yes I realized why I'm here because I wasn't told why I was reassigned & its something I should have known from the beginning so it's funny now that I'm basically slapped in the face with the realization. Bella stands up walking to the coffee pot cup in hand, she fills her cup, then goes to the fridge grabbing the pitcher of tea & walks back to the table, fills the girls glasses sits the pitcher down & continues as she takes her seat. Bella continues, so while I was gone your mother eventually returned to the Shadow Haven, some call it an orphanage & in a way it was, we did take in children that needed a home. Ofcoarse raising them to know about the shadow realms & how to maintain the seal there. Jenna having been thinking & listening asks, Aunt Bella, I know I may be skipping ahead but I have to ask why were you assigned here? Bella lights a smoke & says I can't answer all your questions Jenna, but I can tell you it's because of what your grandmother was & who you will be. Before anyone can ask another question Bella says, Some things have to be learned not taught girls, & even if you don't understand this now, you will. River squeezes Jenna's hand & says we'll learn it together Jenna. Jenna's reply is to just give River a kiss & say ok well do it together, then looks at Bella & says for whatever you did & what you are doing aunt Bella I thank you. Bella smiles & says no worries girl. Both River & Jenna giggle at that, Bella using one of their terms. Taking another drag from her cigarette Bella continues. She says I was told by our parents when your mother returned from college, they kept me informed of everything as far as I'm aware of. But there must have been something they missed because shortly after you were born & I received the picture of your mom holding you River, then word stopped coming. River immediately asks you didn't go find out why? Bella puts her cigarette out, takes another drink of her coffee & says, of course, I did. Bella takes a deep breath & says, sorry River but by the time enough time passed for me to know I needed to go there myself it was to late. Tears filled Bella's eyes running down her cheeks, & says when I arrived all I found were bodies, it was a massacre. She takes a long drink of her coffee then continues, I found two hundred 47 bodies. I know there were two hundred fifty-five people there from my father's last message but I couldn't tell you where they all went. Of course, I searched everywhere, even the chamber with the seal, that at least was still intact. But I did find something that I recognized, one body that of a male. Bella hesitates, lights another cigarette inhaling deeply, then shakily continues. The man was a victim of a Shadow Hunter, his soul was devoured girls. She watches them seeing the fear in their eyes, and says I see you both understand now, something happened to you two last night. The two girls look at each other a moment then River says it came for us, we got away but aren't sure how. Bella smiles as smoke drifts from her nose, & says probably had something to do with a little black cat. Jenna says, we need to know about the cat too please. Bella says, in a moment girls. Then she finishes by saying, that's why I was only concerned about the hunter in your dream River, if you dreamed of it that means it's coming and the little black cat is a friend. Bella finishes her cigarette & says take a break girls we have time, then I'll tell you what I know of Odiewan.

The girls think about it a moment & Jenna finally says, now that I think about it I gotta pee, that gets some giggles. As the girls stand up they do realize this has been difficult for Bella, so they walk over to her & give her a hug & kiss. River says thank you to her & she just nods & whispers softly your both very welcome. The girls head upstairs & as Jenna sits on the toilet she looks at River & asks, what do you think she meant about my grandmother & me? River contemplates that watching Jenna finish up and then sitting on the toilet herself, thinking about the last six months of being here knowing Jenna & the short time she knew her grandmother. Finally River remembers something. As she's finishing up she turns after flushing to Jenna & says, this may be nothing but one of the days you were at school I helped your grandmother carry groceries into the house, after that was done I was just standing there waiting to see if she'd need more help or just some company. Jenna listening intently hopes this will give some answer & shes tearing up thinking about her grandmother. River seeing this takes her hand & walks her out of the bathroom to the bed, they sit down together Jenna watching River. River continues, your grandmother hugged me & said thank you, then said there's tea in the fridge River get us some & come sit with me. After I got our tea I found your grandmother in her favorite chair, I gave her her tea & sat on the couch with mine. It took your grandmother a minute to start talking but when she did she asked me, do you love my Jenna? Jenna hearing this perks up, because at this time of knowing each other they hadn't begun to realize they even had an attraction to each other, Jenna hopes she told her grandmother yes looking back at it now ofcoarse. River blushes a little seeing Jenna's response, Jenna can't help herself & teases her a little, saying you said yes River my grandmother knew you loved me before I did, & sticks her tongue out at her, River being a smart ass takes it as an invitation & licks Jenna's tongue, the two girls giggle a bit. When they stop River continues, I told her I did, & even told her that I was attracted to you. Jenna giggles some more & River blushes a little. Jenna encourages River to continue. River says, you're grandmother just smiled sipped some tea, then she got real serious & said, remember your love for Jenna, it & hers will save you both. Then she leaned back sitting her tea down & closed her eyes. Jenna sniffles a little & says she got really tired the closer the end came. River holds her & after a bit Jenna looks at River gives her a kiss & says thank you River, it doesn't answer the question but I believe grandmother was telling you something. River says I agree, then asks should we get back to Aunt Bella. Jenna always the one to try to make them cheerful says, only if your done licking my tongue, River giggles leaning in & kissing Jenna again.

After a bit they head back downstairs Bella standing in the doorway on the phone they wait, giving her privacy. When Bella's done on the phone she takes a deep breath looks at the girls & decides to tease them seeing they are in good spirits she says, that must've been a good bathroom break you two you both look very refreshed & ready to continue. Jenna blushes & is speechless, but River blushes some just says you can't really time a bathroom break, Aunt Bella. Bella just says mhm & asks shall we continue? The girls grab tea & take a seat, Bella lights a cigarette & takes a seat as well. Bella says ok so we were at Odiewan. Bella takes a slow drag from her cigarette remembering her experience with Odiewan, smiling at the happy memories. She says Odiewan was my childhood companion, I don't remember when he came into my life but he was by my side until your mother left for college, he didn't really ask or really tell me but said, Bella, I have to go with your sister now, of course, I was heartbroken & asked why, he just answered me in the way he always does & said, it's not for your sister it's for you Bella, I know it hurts, it hurts me as well, but you'll understand when she comes into your life. I didn't understand River until I met you but when I arrived to pick you up from the state after your parents death I immediately knew why. River's mind is filling up with questions, she begins to fidget, Jenna puts her hand on her thigh helping calm her nerves, taking her hand River focuses & calms a little. Bella continues, I could sense my old friend on you, he'd been beside you your whole life up to that point. Bella drinks some coffee then continues, I couldn't understand & still don't know why I didn't see him, but you remember when it was time to leave your house after getting your things I hesitated at the front door? River says I remember, I thought you were just saying goodbye in your own way. Bella sniffles a little & says, I said my goodbyes at the funeral River, what I was doing was looking for Odiewan. River nods, then says, in my dream, he asked if I remembered him, Aunt Bella I don't remember him, do you know why? Bella shakes her head no, blowing out her last drag & putting out her cigarette. Bella says you should remember him though, from what I know of Odiewan he probably knows why you don't. After a short silence Jenna asks, what is he really? Bella sips the last of her coffee & gets up to grab more, saying sorry Jenna I don't know that either. But what I do know is this, he taught me about being a Valkyrie & had me trained by someone he just called Fey. Fey was a tall man, black hair lean build, & for 10 years he never seemed to age. I remember he was very polite, very serious & stern during training. Bella sighs with a smile on her face, the girls seeing that smile at least once a day on each other's faces giggle at Bella. Bella immediately gets serious & eyes them, the girls look sheepish a moment then Bella laughs, she says you two know that smile & your right, Fey trained me until I was sixteen. Bella sips her coffee & instead of lightning a cigarette reaches for her lighter & flicks it between her fingers, eyes glossing over remembering. The girls wait in silence & watch their aunt. Finally she speaks, her voice soft & full of fondness, she says on my sixteenth birthday, I beat Fey for the first time sparring, when I realized what had happened I was so happy I fell onto him laughing from the excitement. He laid there under me waiting for me to settle down when I did I looked into his eyes, just then Bella remembering his eyes pauses in shock, she realizes then that they were cat eyes. She takes a moment piecing that together & realizes that she'll need to ask Odiewan but

Odiewan may have been Fey & she doesn't remember seeing either of them at the same time. After a moment she realizes the girls have noticed her pause, she chuckles & says sorry girls just reliving the moment. The girls are smiling getting the idea of where this is going or where it seems to be going, Bella eyes them a moment a little smile on her face deciding what to tell them or not too. She sips her coffee lights a cigarette sighs the exhale says, I looked into his eyes young girl & all being held by my mentor & now the man I realized I was attracted to, so very nervous as I was I kissed him & he did he kiss me back. She takes another drag off her smoke looking at the girls she says, he looked at me & said Bella first of all happy birthday, second of all that was the best kiss of my life, of coarse at sixteen I was very happy to hear that, now I'm just glad he was protecting my heart. She sighs & says the third thing he said to me was, congratulations Bella your training is now complete, all that's left is experience & knowledge that comes from experience. She sniffles we said our goodbyes I never seen him again, Odiewan was by my side always as I said until your mom left for college. Bella drinks some coffee & then says yes, I asked him many times over the years what he was, and every time I asked him he had the same reply, if you can explain to me Bella how the answer to that question can make our friendship better, & how that knowledge will improve your life I will gladly tell you.

Bella smiles of course I never had that answer. There's some silence & the girls drink some tea. Then Jenna says Aunt Bella, your trainer was Fey? River looks at Jenna wide eyes even wider, surprise & revelation, River says, dad's name was Carl Fey, & mom was Willow Fey! She turns to Bella & says that can't be by accident! Odiewan was looking out for me I just can't remember. Bella smiles & says & to use his words "congratulations, there's nothing more I can teach you". Bella laughs & says River, Jenna I love you both dearly but it's true there nothing more I can teach you, go to the library when your ready, see what you can learn there about Shadow Haven, I can tell you what I know but I havnt been there in twelve years. Before you go you both better come back & say goodbye to me. All three girls start tearing up & the hugging begins, after that the girls get some things together & head out, sadness & happiness heavy on all three. As the car pulls away Bella thinks to herself, Odiewan you sneaky bustard, full of surprises. She stands there a moment just staring off thinking about things, then she remembers the last thing Odiewan said to her & her heart catches. She feels the presence of the Shadow Hunter, turning around she sees it, drifting in & out of the shadows cast by the doorframe leading into the small hallway towards the kitchen. Bella takes a deep breath closing the front door behind her....the house goes dark.

Chapter 7

Nullsoul waits for his moment patiently not allowing his full essence into the realm, he has learned the hard way to have patience. He does think to himself, both targets are here if I could take them both the Unseen Ones would surely see his value. After considering this he realizes that they cleared his target, the Shadow Girl is not his to hunt, also she has protection far to powerful for him so he waits. Listening to his target tell her story he realizes they have a connection, furthermore, somehow the Shadow Girl is connected as well. No! He says to himself, focus they are nothing accept prey. He keeps himself focused & finally his time comes, the targets back is to him, he moves into the relm getting ready to take her. Suddenly she turns facing him, he senses no fear, no dread, catching her scent he gets that feeling again. Then surprisingly she steps forward closing the door. Bella looks at it taking it in she realizes she can't read it, no body language no telltale signs of whether it's confident or not. Then she says, fuck it I'm Valkyrie, no shield, no FEAR!! As Bella rushes the hunter a four foot long slightly curved blade materializes in her right hand, glowing & pulsing in white & silver. As Bella strikes she's both surprised & impressed, the hunter moved not completely but enough to save him from what she thought would be a deadly blow. As the prey advances he knows something is wrong, in all of Nullsoul's time hunting prey none have willingly or confidently challenged him. Suddenly he sees her weapon of choice & knows for certain something is wrong, it is swirling white & silver same as that... he dodges not even registering she'd not only covered the distance to him but also swung in less than a second. The doorframe explodes, wood splinters igniting, and Bella relentlessly pursues the hunter not letting him regain balance. The hunter is still dangerous though, recognizing what the target is doing he fazes, falling through the floor, Bella pursues, stomping down hard, the impact blowing the windows out of the house. Hitting the cement basement floor Bella doesn't see the hunter, then she feels him. Spinning around the sword in an arc, she brings up her right leg, the hunter catches her leg ducking to the left her swing misses. The hunter moves pinning her to the wall, Bella struggles but the hunter is too strong. Nullsoul is surprised, he thought this was going to be more difficult, but he has her, he opens his maw wide, and as he begins to take her essence, his prey turns her head & says, Valkyrie, you abomination. Then there's a white light he's in pain curled up on the floor, he thinks the Unseen Ones are punishing him. After a moment nothing is happening, the pain is gone. Nullsoul smells smoke and hears an odd noise, loud & coming closer. He gets up, no sign of the prey, he hears the Unseen Ones in his mind, you succeed, hide, recover your strength you are not finished. Nullsoul listens to them, as he turns to go he sees his prey's sword on the cement floor, before he can think to reach for it the small black cat walks over & puts its right paw on the blade. The small black cat speaks into Nullsoul's mind using the Shadow Girl's voice, it is not low noon yet hunter, will you be testing me? Nullsoul already knows better & he has orders so he retreats to regain his strength & await orders.

River & Jenna get in the car, they see Aunt Bella at the front door watching them. The girls wave, as they drive away Jenna says, she looked sad River. River looks at her saying, she loves us, Jenna, & she's letting us go off on our own to face who knows what? Jenna nods putting her left hand on River's right thigh, after a moment Jenna says, River she didn't tell us what your mother did that was so terrible. River sighs & says, maybe to protect me, maybe because she didn't know how even possibly it's because it doesn't affect our situation. Either way, Aunt Bella was a great help. Jenna says, your right there are so many reasons & we just don't know, I think though if it would have helped us she would have said. The girls are quiet for the rest of the ride, when they get out of the car River puts her hood up over her black hair covering her large eyes. Jenna used to this walks around the car & takes her hand waiting for River to be ready to be in public. Surprising Jenna, River immediately starts walking towards the library doors, Jenna smiles thinking to herself that at least some good has come from what's happening, she is proud of River's newfound confidence. When they get to the door River teases her a bit & says, I see that smile, Jenna giggles & River looks at her & says thank you. Jenna still smiling grabs the door & says we got this. As they walk into the library River & Jenna stop for a moment looking around, they realize this could be a big task. River who's been thinking about this since they got here remembers that they spent their sixteenth birthday here, & that their seventeenth birthday is only two months away. River leans over & whispers to Jenna, Happy birthday love. Jenna suddenly remembers smiles & says you too River. Both knowing that two months from now they may not have the chance. The two girls walk up to the front desk seeing old Miss Kyle still there, they both over the last half year have tried to guess her age but neither have been brave enough to ask her, she is a kind old lady though & always helped the girls. As they approach Jenna as always says hello Miss Kyle. Miss Kyle looks up & smiles, helloooo Jenna & River good to see you girls again! Jenna says you too Miss Kyle. Miss Kyle asks how things have been & Jenna talks to her, and River trying to be patient. Finally, Miss Kyle looks over & asks, still hiding that beautiful face River? By now River's impatience is almost too much to bear, she knows Miss Kyle means well but she knows Jenna & herself don't have much time. Taking a deep breath River says, yes Miss Kyle, the world still isn't ready to see me, as has always been her answer, a game she & Jenna play. This time Miss Kyle surprises them both saying, the world may never be River, but you have sweet Jenna to adore you. Both girls shocked & surprised because that's not miss Kyle's normal response. Miss Kyle doest wait, she says so what can I help you two with today? Jenna clears her throat, & says we need information on Shadow Haven in Portland please, Miss Kyle smiles & says follow me, please. After following her to the back she sits them down infront of a computer inside a booth & taps the space key on the keyboard, when the screen lights up it displays a news paper article with the headline, Shadow Haven

Orphanage closes today in Portland Oregon. The two girls just sit in silence a moment & miss Kyle says, I'll leave you two too it then. Jenna looks at her saying, how? Miss Kyle just smiles & walks away. River calls out thank you to her but she just keeps walking. Putting their heads together River & Jenna start whispering, how'd she know River? River tells Jenna, I don't remember how long we were upstairs, but when we came back down aunt Bella was on the phone, she could have done this. Jenna thinks about it & says that's probably it, ok ready? River nods & they turn to the computer.

In the neither realm Nullsoul sits & gathers his strength, the prey may have only struck him once with her sword but it was devastating. Thinking back on it besides the white & silver swirls he remembers another thing about the preys blade, crimson or to him blood, he even realized the metal flowed with this color. After some more thought on this he realizes, he did not win the hunt, he did not absorb the preys essence. Confused Nullsoul can't understand why the Unseen Ones said he had succeeded. The prey vanished not dead. As he ponders this he senses a portal opening, immediately to his feet he's ready for a fight. The portal opening appears infront of him, unlike any he's seen before. Smaller then normal & its color is off. Instead of black it's Grey, not knowing what to expect he readies himself. What emerges from the portal he recognizes only having seen one once before, stepping from the portal is a small creature. Wearing black robes covering its face & body, approximately three feet tall, Nullsoul seeing it's just a courier for the Unseen Ones relaxes sitting back down. The small courier approaches him & he presents his right hand, the courier sniffs Nullsoul taking in his scent. The courier seeming to have found the recipient of his message, stands up straight & holds out it's left hand, opening it palm up. Laying on the three-fingered palm Nullsoul sees a small metallic object, engraved on it is a Valkyrie, panic partially fills Nullsoul & he takes his feet, Nullsoul is getting tired of this, since the Unseen Ones have recruited him he's learned fear & he doesn't like it. When he lets out a growl the courier doesn't react but the Unseen Ones do, falling to the ground in pain he hears their voice in his head. You will respect our courier! As the pain subsides Nullsoul receives his new orders, getting to his feet he bows his head to the courier showing respect, then takes what he has learned to be a lighter from the small courier's hand. The courier immediately turns, summons its portal & vanishes. Nullsoul readies himself, and along with his new orders came something he can't understand. Do not engage the Shadow Girl in combat, deliver the message & leave. Why such an order? He knows they want her dead, he is happy though, the Unseen Ones gave him permission to feed on the Shadow Girl's mate. Nullsoul is grateful as he is hungry.

As the girls read the headline of the paper it says: Shadow Haven shuts down June 21st 1988. Bella said twelve years, Jenna sighs saying, think we'll find anything? River says, just what was public probably. As they search the records they find what mostly Aunt Bella said, they took in orphans, but most recently before closing they had started taking on orphans needing some medical treatment. After they read on at the bottom of the article it says closed by Bella J. Seraph. River says, she didn't mention that. Jenna says it's OK probably not important, besides as far as anyone knows she'd be the last survivor of the staff. River saying you're right, sees a tab saying related articles, as she clicks it Jenna is writing down the address to Shadow Haven. When she looks up she sees the article River is reading, claims of hidden secrets, government investigations & mentions of conspiracy & cover-ups. Jenna says love ignore those, even if there's some truth to them how will we know. River sighs & says your right, just before closing the page Jenna says look here pointing at the screen. River reads, a survivor of Shadow Haven, as they read that article they also find out he refused to be interviewed & whatever he told the authorities they refused to make public. River sees his name, and Jenna writes down his name we can find his address in the phone book. As Jenna writes it down she mumbles his name, Timothy Went, River chuckles seeing a joke & says hopefully not insane. The girls giggle a bit then Jenna says I gotta pee, you coming or looking up his address? River gives her a quick kiss & says I'll be ok...um just hurry Jenna. Jenna smiles be back before your done & runs to the bathroom, River finds Timothy's phone number even an address, thinking why's he listed? Then she brushes it off thinking what do I know?

Chapter 8

Nullsoul watches patiently from the void between realms, he's disgusted by them, touching, and putting their mouths together, and he starts growing a hatred for them building. He actually feels the desire to kill them, not for food but for pleasure, as he ponders this feeling he sees his chance. The Shadow Girl's mate is leaving her side, he knows he needs to hurry, if the Shadow Girl finds him feeding she may attack & he cannot risk failure. He follows the mate, and seeing she's going into a room without an exit he gets the hunters rush & pursues. Once inside he sees her sitting on a bowl of water, hearing something leak from her, disgusted again he fully enters the room. River feels it, the Shadow Hunter, immediately she gets up to run to Jenna. On the way panicking hoping she gets there in time. Nullsoul moves, rushing the bathroom stall, ripping the door from the hinges throwing it across the bathroom its impact is so great it's driven into the wall behind a mirror. Then...he sees nothing! No mate, no sign of any life, & all he can smell is her waste, he roars. River reaching the bathroom door slowly opens it she senses him on the other side, though afraid she must know if Jenna is OK. As she slowly opens the door a shadow moves by in the light, and then there's a crash, as she looks around the door she sees the stall door embedded in the mirror. When she hears his roar her head & eyes snap back to the hunter, & she's heartbroken knowing she was too late, thinking of her options she remembers telling Jenna, we run no more. Run no more! She screams in her head, slowly pushing the door open. As she enters Nullsoul feels her presence, burying his rage over his lost meal he looks over his shoulder head turning slowly, just showing his eye over the quivering mass of shadow form that would be his shoulder. He feels for the lighter & brings it from the pouch he'd placed it in slowly turning towards the Shadow Girl. Once facing her he sees & senses no fear, the look on her face says to him she's making a stand. He knows he has to hurry to follow his orders. Slowly he raises his right hand, lighting the lighter he positions it by the bottom edge between his forefinger & thumb, or what passes for them. There he holds it, flame burning & the engraving of the Valkrye facing the Shadow Girl. He sees her eyes move to the lighter and holds it a moment thinking the message is delivered, whatever it means. He goes to toss the lighter at her feet before it can leave his hand he's buried in the brick wall inside the stall, blows relentlessly pounding his head, and he fills himself losing consciousness. River sees the Shadow Hunter raise his right hand slowly & he's holding something, as she begins to recognize it her breath catches in her lungs, & her heart begins to pound as she feels tears in her eyes. Thinking to herself, no, no, no! This can't be, no. But as he holds it up & lights it, before she even sees the engraving she knows. As her mind screams Aunt Bella! She feels energy inside her, extremely powerful she feels it's limitless. Her jade green eyes light up, her vision changes & all she sees is the Shadow Hunter's dark energy, her skin comes to life, purple energy lines outlined with blue swirling through her like bioluminescence. Then she's calm no emotions, no desires. Save one kill cathululips, & she moves hovering above the floor so fast he can't respond. She drives him into the cinderblock wall inside the stall with her right fist, without hesitation she's on him, beating him relentlessly....then he's gone, falling through the floor. She stands there black hair covering her face, & the tears come.

Nullsoul hits the ground with a thud, The Unseen Ones not caring he's nearly dead. They wait for him to awaken. When Nullsoul begins to regain consciousness he feels pain, in his head, slowly he raises his hands to his face & realizes he can't see them. Cautiously he touches his face screaming in agony, warm sticky fluids covering his hand and running through his finger. He roars in outrage never has his body been beaten so badly. Just as he starts to calm himself pain begins again, he curls on the floor crying out until his voice only allows a whisper. After a time the pain stops from The Unseen Ones, as consciousness comes & goes he tries to figure out why they are punishing him. He did not fail! His mind screams in rage, then more pain. When it stops he hears them. You were told not to engage The Shadow Girl! Nullsoul doesn't dare contradict them, instead, he lays there in silence choking on his own black fluids. After a moment The Unseen Ones speak to him again. You failed us! By engaging her you allowed her to access her power! Nullsoul thinks this over maybe they are right, maybe. The only other option was to try & feed on the mate after, but he couldn't see of any way that would work. Then The Unseen

Ones speak again. You will be banished once more! If you manage to survive, perhaps you will become stronger in some way. After a moment of silence, Nullsoul feels the portal around him, then he falls. After hitting the ground he falls unconscious again, when he is awake he can see again but very little. He tries to move but cannot, taking a moment he realizes he is upright. He struggles some more but in vain, whatever is holding him he can't break free of it. He looks around moving his damaged eyes, doesn't quite recognize this place but perhaps it's his damaged eyes, he sees as much of his own black blood as anything else. Then he hears someone approach, not sure from where as he realizes he can only hear from his right ear. The creature steps in front of him, he doesn't recognize it, so as it studies him he does the same in return. He notes that it has some sort of armored skin, scales he believes is the word, green with red stripes, a small spade-shaped muzzle & multiple irises, red, green, & a color he doesn't know. Before he can notice more the creature raises its right hand making a fist, Nullsoul expects the creature is going to strike him but instead, it extends one finger unsheathing a razor-sharp claw, the creature slices one of his tentacles from his face, Nullsoul doesn't cry out thinking that's what the creature wants. Holding the tentacle in its left hand it eyes Nullsoul as it opens its mouth dropping the tentacle inside. As it chews it watches Nullsoul, when the creature finishes chewing it swallows, smiles & begins to carve Nullsoul's chest open. It does take long & Nullsoul loses consciousness.

On the way to the toilet Jenna is happy a big grin on her face, this is the first time in public that River has been brave enough to be alone, even in the library. She knows still she should hurry not knowing how long River can handle it. Jenna gets to the toilet closes the stall door dropping her pants. As she pees she sighs giggling a little, River & her tea she thinks to herself, my bladder is always so full! That's all the time she can spare to think of that, suddenly she smells the putrid stank of the Shadow Hunter, & immediately the stall door vanishes. Jenna feels disoriented for just a moment & then realizes she's in the backseat of a moving car. She looks forward just as a man she doesn't know that's driving the car begins to look over his right shoulder at her. Just as he's about to say hello to her he gets a sneaker to the back of the head, foot still inside. Jenna kicked him so hard that his head hit the glass in the driver's side door spiderwebbing it. Jenna doesn't even pull up her pants instead she stands over the seat grabbing a handful of his hair, she slams the glass again with his skull. The man in severe pain at this point manages to pull the car over & stops it on the curb, screaming I'm here to help! Jenna hearing this let's go & says fuck off! She opens the back passenger side door and slides off the seat putting her feet on the ground trying to take a step forward she falls on her face, pants & undies still around her ankles. She grunts at herself realizing immediately what's happened, she rolls over sitting on her little bare ass in the grass & grabs the waistline of her pants & panties as she's standing pulling them up the man walks around the back of the car holding his head, blood in his blonde hair & on his hand. Jenna looks up at him still ready for a fight, when he sees her still getting her pants up he immediately turns around & says my most sincerest apologies, Miss Vella. Jenna hearing him call her by her last name & his politeness is thrown off guard a little & buttoning her pants asks how do you know my name? The man slightly looks back seeing her pants are on fully turns around & says maybe this will help, your aunt Bella called me approximately six hours ago, & yes I am, he looks around a bit then says whispers, a watchers of shadow. He offers her his hand saying Samuel Nigeus, pleased to meet you, Miss Vella. She eyes him a moment not accepting his hand says good for you Samuel, knowing where she is in Wheeler she steps right past him heading back to the library to her River. Samuel not giving up says it will be faster back to River if I drive you, mam. Jenna stops, taking a deep breath turns around & says, first my name is Jenna. Second I'm driving. Seeing the look on her face Samuel decides against arguing, besides with a concussion which he's sure he has it's a bad idea to drive, he reaches into his right pants pocket & tosses her the car keys & says we should hurry. Jenna says there's no we Samuel, You'll find your car at the library. As Jenna is opening the driver's side door Samuel says, I'd be ok with that accept two things mi.. Jenna, one The Shadow Hunter, even if you just activate Captain Human shield I can help you. He sees her smile a little at his joke & thinks good we are getting to a better place. Jenna looks at him & asks, what's two Samuel? He sighs & says, unfortunately, something has happened to your aunt Bella & the police are looking for you both & with this, he reaches into the left back pocket of his jeans & produces credentials she doesn't recognize, I can make all of the authorities go away in short you need me, Jenna, as much as the rest of us need you & River. Jenna thinks about it for a second looking at him doubtful, then says don't make me regret this. As she's getting in she hears him saying I won't my head can't take that twice! As they drive back to the library she asks, Samuel are you the one that saved me? Samuel says yes, I opened a vortex for you short teleportation through the current realm, then he stammers a little & says I'm sorry I literally caught you with your pants down. Jenna not sure if he's flirting or just trying to use humor says you got your one look at my naughty bits Samuel I hope you enjoyed yourself, consider it my way of saying thank you for saving my life. The whole time Jenna was saying this feeling a little guilty since only River ever gets to see her naked. Samuel looks at her a moment, his wisdom seeming to defy his age since he looks to Jenna to be about twenty, and says I didn't see anything naughty Jenna you & River have nothing to worry about. Jenna blushes a little but decides not to say anything more. When they get to the library Samuel jumps out of the car & she watches him run around to the driver's side & pulling a gun from under his black jacket opens her door, he looks at her seriously & says we'll both go but you stay behind me. Jenna looks at him & laughs, his confused look amuses her as well. After she stops laughing as she's getting out of the car Samuel asks her what's so funny? Jenna looks at him seriously now & says, your amazing Samuel everything id except from a good guy, but you've obviously never seen a Shadow Hunter before or you'd know that gun & you're big heart isn't enough to protect shit. Jenna says I'm sorry, I've just been through a lot & I'm worried, she tears up a little, he reaches out to put a hand on her shoulder, Jenna steps back & glares at him shaking her head mean look in her eye. Samuel raises his hands & says sorry & understood Jenna I'll follow you. Jenna heads straight to the bathroom doing her best not to cry knowing if River got there in time & her ability to sense The Shadow Hunter....she stops thinking telling herself ohhh no, not till I see it. When they get to the bathroom she hesitates & Samuel steps forward & using a soft voice says I'll look for you Jenna, she wraps her arms around her torso sniffles & nods. Samuel nods back & steps up to the door readying himself he slowly opens it, as he looks inside he sees there's a gash in the floor from the door to the middle stall, & inside that a destroyed toilet, wall, & some sort of black liquid everywhere. That he kinda recognizes he thinks to himself looks like blood splatter, but the rest of this....I have no idea, then he hears a sniffle from inside the bathroom he opens the door a little more & sees a dark-haired girl sitting on the floor arms crossed in front of herself head down crying. Samuel is immediately excited, he thinks to himself, she is alive! Somehow River survived, he's about to step in then stops himself he looks back at Jenna & nods with his head in the direction of the bathroom & steps back holding the door. Jenna is confused but takes a deep breath & peeks around the door, seeing what Samuel seen & more importantly...River! She rushes in dropping to the floor pulling River close telling her how much she loves her.

River stands there, cathululips blood dripping from her fist. Stunned at what just happened, not just her transformation, but that she was capable of that much violence. Breathing shakily she takes a step back, & sees her aunt's lighter. Tears fill her eyes as she bends down & picks it up as she holds it she collapses in grief crying again. Her mind goes back to the first time she saw her aunt Bella, River had been at home the day it happened as she was already legally an adult, but that didn't prepare her for the knock on the door & the news that came with it. A policeman was there & when she opened the door she knew it was bad news the moment she saw his face. He looked at her & said sorry to bother you mam but are you the daughter of Carl & Willow Fey? She thought to herself who else would I be I'm in their house, head down hiding her large jade eyes she quietly said yes officer. He took a deep breath & said I'm sorry to inform you that their car was in an accident on the freeway &...well I'm sorry they didn't survive. River not really being close to either of them nodded & said thank you, officer, is there anything I need to do? He said yes when you can please go to the morgue & claim their bodies. He handed her a card & said phone number & address. River said thank you & the officer left, she read the card & saw the hours, the morgue was closed until morning since it was after five, she put the card in her sweater pocket not sure exactly how to handle this. River ate dinner, showered & went to bed, at four a.m. she woke up to the doorbell. Groaning to herself she grabbed her shorts & tank top heading downstairs, at the front door she grabbed one of her many zipp-up hoodies to hide her eyes & looked through the peephole. She didn't recognize the woman outside, she had red hair, was taller than River & was smoking a cigarette. River finally was brave enough to say who is it after the doorbell rang again thinking this woman wasn't just going away. Surprisingly the woman's voice was soothing even through the door as she said, hello I hope this is River Fey, I'm Bella Seraph & I know you may not know me but believe it or not I'm Willow's older sister. River stood there a moment not believing her but still wondering if she'd heard of her before, while she was thinking this over a picture slid under the door. After she bent over & picked it up she looked at it, it was a picture of her mom & this woman, her mom was very young, but this woman looked the same. River slid her picture back under the door & said that was good but my mother was young & if you're older then she you must have a great surgeon before the woman could respond River said you can go now & if you're here in one hour I will just call the police. River walked away from the front door & went & crashed on the couch. In the morning River called the morgue to let them know she was coming, the nice woman on the phone said, ok River then asked if she knew about her mother's older sister. Then explained that they had called the number in her mother's medical file but there was no answer. River asked the woman her name & she said Bella J. Seraph, River hesitated a moment then said yes she'll be coming with me. The nice lady said that's good see you when you get here & hung up. River shook her head & ate breakfast, & cleaned up when she was ready went to the front door & opened it across the street was Bella sitting on the hood of her car. River pulled her hood down locked & closed her door & went across the street & stood in front of the woman head down, holding the card to the morgue up to her said, You're driving. River sitting there crying thinking how she lost the only two people in her life that she loved didn't notice the bathroom door open nor the man looking inside. She didn't notice Jenna or her cry of River! As Jenna ran to her holding her, when River looked up into Jenna's eyes, all she could say was from now until forever.

Chapter 9

Nullsoul is standing in a forest, he doesn't remember how he got here but recognizes it from before the Unseen Ones took him. As he tries to remember how he came to be here he listens to the world, birds chirping, tree branches creaking in the wind. Even a squirrel cracking some nuts. He feels his hunger, he's hungrier than he's ever been, he begins hunting. After some time he catches a scent powerful & strong, vaguely fulmilure. In his hunger Nullsoul doesn't hesitate, he pursues. He stalks it to a clearing, in the clearing stands a large building three stories tall on one side is a large four-car garage with a road overgrown with weeds leading to it, behind the building is just more forest. Nullsoul stops surprised, this is his beginning, where he learned to hunt! He begins to step forward & then stops seeing the prey he had been pursuing. It stands there, white tennis shoes, black jeans & sweater, on the sweater is a heart with a banner saying Until forever. He looks up to see his prey's eyes, all he sees is head down, hood up black hair coming out the sides. Then he hears this in his mind, a soft female voice says, this could be low noon Hunter, choose wisely. Nullsoul is in instant panic he turns to run, as he runs into the trees he slams into a thick branch hitting his head, before he hits the ground he's out.

Nullsoul snaps awake, he was dreaming he realizes. He lets his head lower & tries opening his eyes, they open barely caked with his dried blood. He still feels the fear & panic, he feels the hatred from this. I will KILL THEM! He makes this vow to himself. But how? I must escape this place & like it or not I need The Unseen Ones. He begins hating them too, needing them means he's weak. His thoughts are broken when he hears a soft moaning beside him, forcing one eye slightly open he looks. Beside him is something he recognizes, it's from the realm he was first banished to. Nullsoul feels excitement, if this one recognizes him it will fear him, dread him & he can feed. He hears the others approaching, Nullsoul keeps his head down looking through the lids of his barely one-open eye. They approach Nullsoul grabbing his head, he thinks to himself, appear weak they may not feed on me. After a moment his head is released, flopping back to his chest. The creatures say something he doesn't understand and thankfully walk away from him. As they approach the other tied next to him he watches in anticipation, if it awakens & sees him & recognizes him it's all he'll need. As the creatures approach the newest food, they ponder it. To them, they see something weak & pathetic, four small fingers on each hand, feet with tiny toes not even long enough to be useful. They decide it will just be eaten quickly, however they like to play with their food. One of the creatures slaps it across its small face to wake it, it works the pathetic little creature wakes up panicked. Not enough for Nullsoul to feed on but a start, he watches hoping they'll get it scared enough. The creatures play with it taking a small piece of flesh, eating a finger. Not enough though, Nullsoul knows he must do something before it dies, he needs its dread. Nullsoul knowing its language decides to try this, he says to it hoping he's speaking loud enough. Wishaki! Look at me The Shadow Hunter! It works the little Wishaki turns its head looking at Nullsoul. As its eyes widen Nullsoul knows its dread, Nullsoul says to the Wishaki, yes give me your dread & I will kill them all, or they can eat you ALIVE! it works between Nullsoul & it being eaten alive the Wishaki's dread flows, & Nullsoul feeds.

As Nullsoul feeds his body is restored he must drain the Wishaki completely, he senses the creatures stirring. They see what's happening but don't understand it. Nullsoul thinks to himself good! You will know my power! Done with feeding he rips himself free of the feeding post they had tied him to, only one thought…kill them all! He lashes out using the barriers in the realm to teleport instantly to his next prey. In the end, it was just pure carnage, & hatred that drove Nullsoul. His hunger already satisfied by the Wishaki's essence. Nullsoul slaughtering everything. The creatures that fed on him, & their food he left none alive. When he finished he scanned the area carefully making sure none remained. Then he sensed a portal, and when it opened he was joyed, seeing it he knew The Unseen Ones were inviting his return. Stepping through the portal Nullsoul knew not what to expect, they punish him even when he was not at fault however he had found a new determination & he would endure their punishment. Once on the other side in The Unseen Ones' chamber, Nullsoul kneeled waiting. When The Unseen Ones spoke to him he didn't know how to take what they said however he knew they were happy with him. Nullsoul received his new orders fueled by hatred & was sent back to the realm of The Shadow Girl, this time with permission to hunt her & all her allies, but with a word of caution. Be patient the Unseen Ones said, follow, learn your prey & your time to strike! Impatience will be your death....Nullsoul listens to this & considers it. Finally, he reaches the conclusion they are correct remembering his experiences being eaten alive.

Chapter 10

While River & Jenna take a moment to catch up Samuel looks around the bathroom taking it all in, he can't fathom what must've happened here. Blood he thinks is everywhere in the stall & on the floor including poor River. But the gash in the floor, the toilet gone, he sees small pieces of porcelain strewn about like the toilet exploded. When he sees the girls going to the sink he sees the stall door. He looks closer, it's buried halfway into the cinderblock, he shakes his head, wondering if Bella knew what he'd be getting into & if she had someone better to call who was more equipped than himself to handle this. As he's contemplating this Jenna is washing River's hair in the sink, River asks Jenna, who's the lost-looking beach boy? Jenna says that's Samuel Nigeus, he says Aunt Bella sent him, he's…ok but not very good at this however he takes credit for saving my life. River turns her head in the sink eyeing him, she asks Jenna why he has blood in his hair. Jenna chuckles a little shyly saying he ran into a car window, Samuel says you'd be proud of her River it was her ninja kitten-kicking skills that ran my head into the said window. River chuckles a little & says good work, Jenna. Jenna smiles & says let's get the hairbrush from our bag, did you leave it in the computer booth?

Before River can answer the door opens a crack & they hear Miss Kyle ask, girls may I come in? They look at each other & begin giggling, Samuel raises his pistol, and Jenna looks at him & says down boy, she's a friend. Samuel looking humble lowers his pistol & River says yes Miss Kyle come in. Opening the door the rest of the way she comes in carrying a tray, on it a plate with two tuna sandwiches & two cups of hot black tea, & draping from her left arm the girl's bag. Both girls are shocked as she walks over gentle smile on her old tired face & sets the tray on the sink, and then hands River their bag. Before they can speak Miss Kyle wraps her arms around them hugging them both sighs & says I knew you girls would prevail, but I still worried. In shock still, River looks up slowly into Miss Kyle's eyes & asks how did you know? Miss Kyle takes River's face between her hands & gently kisses her forehead, & says it doesn't matter girls my story ends here & yours are just beginning. Miss Kyle tears up a little & says I love you both, then collecting herself turns to Samuel & says, Samuel, he straightens up hearing a grandmother's voice. Miss Kyle continues, watch over them, help them, but remember this is their story they will decide it. With that she walks out of the bathroom, River & Jenna chuckle at each other, devouring the food Miss Kyle brought them.

When the girls finish eating River looks at her sweater on the floor, Jenna seeing this takes her sweater off and handing it to River, she smiles shyly in thanks & puts it on pulling the hood up over her eyes. River grabs the tray & Jenna gets the door when Jenna looks to see what Samuel is doing he's grabbing River's sweater, Jenna says, what are you doing creepy? Samuel looks at her realizing she's speaking to him, he says sorry I realize how this looks but it's evidence & we need to keep people from this. River & Jenna look at him suspiciously, River says you better be burning that & I want to watch or you can stay away from us starting now. Samuel says you can light the fire River, I assure you my intentions are pure. River looks at Jenna & asks her as she's walking away, where did Aunt Bella dig this guy up? Jenna says not sure, looking over her shoulder at Samuel says but he better start talking. When they get to the front desk Miss Kyle is nowhere to be seen, so they set the tray on the desk with a note saying thank you Miss Kyle, signed R. & J. Heading to the door River says Samuel now you tell us. Samuel nods & says no problem. He starts by saying, I'm with the Watchers of Shadow, but to be honest, I don't know why Bella called me, & she left out that you two were being pursued by a Shadow Hunter. He says as far as knowing your aunt she saved my life when I was five, something set my home on fire, I never learned what but your aunt killed it & pulled me from the fire, she couldn't save my parents. From there she sent me to my family, my father's brother but he had no interest in raising me, The Watchers of Shadow were keeping an eye on me & after a year took me from my uncle & raised me in Indiana. As far as my abilities are concerned, short-range teleport inside the current realm, & with these, he reaches in his inner coat pocket, I can find you two and even sense what's going on around you, that's how I knew to save Jenna. Jenna quickly snatches the pictures from his hand, looking at them the girls tear up, they figure Aunt Bella took them, the two girls sitting in Jenna's grandmother's gazebo. Samuel seeing their reaction just says keep them I can use other ways to teleport the two of you if need be. The girls put the pictures in their bag & he continued, yes I have training as an agent, however, I'm not experienced you two know that & I admit it. He sighs running his left hand through bloody blonde hair wincing, he says honestly Bella could have sent you two someone better. The two girls just look at him a moment then Jenna remembering, says you said Aunt Bella was in trouble what did you mean? He looks at them & says I'm not completely sure what has happened but the police scanner in my car said there was a fire & mentioned your address I don't know more because I came directly to you to sensing your danger, he looks concerned I can't sense your aunt Bella haven't been able to sense her before I got to Wheeler. The girls don't think they move to their car & River heads straight home.

River driving gets them home in record time, surprisingly Samuel kept up. Pulling up the street they see two fire trucks & four police cars, the girls tear up still seeing the smoke. When they pull up River doesn't get out she pulls her hood lower, Jenna kisses her & says I'll talk to them. As Jenna gets out of the car & starts heading to the nearest police officer Samuel parks behind River, getting out of his car he just watches. The police officer Jenna approaches and recognizes her, knowing she's one of the people they need to find he steps up to her & immediately says you need to explain where you've been. Jenna not liking this immediately gets defensive & says my aunt's house is burned down

& you're demanding to know where I've been?! River seeing her love having a problem starts to light up, purple bioluminescent lights spiraling through her skin, before the blue outlines show up Samuel speaks into the partially open driver's side window, and he calmly says. Allow me, Miss Fey. River looks at him not sure what he'll do but knowing if she does anything it will be bad for all involved, so she calms down watching Samuel. As Samuel approaches the officer tries to grab Jenna, but she's too fast for him & backs up. The officer turns signaling for assistance, when he turns around Samuel is standing there. Panicking as a new face is in his he reaches for his pistol, Samuel moving very fast puts his left hand on the officer's gun in its holster, right hand brings his credentials up to the officer's face. The other four cops point their pistols at Samuel, Samuel remaining calm says, with respect, you're all done here. Samuel waits for the officer to read his credentials, the officer getting a blank look on his face says I'll have to check this with my captain. Samuel removes his hand from the officer's pistol & puts his credentials away, says understood. The other officers stand down, and one of the other officers says those two will still need to come with us. Samuel looks that officer in the eyes & says, they are in my custody the only way you can take them this day is with my death. Samuel doesn't flinch locking eyes with the officer. After what seems like forever the officer who went to check with his captain jumps from his squad car & says, captain's orders we leave now. The other officer looking confused decides to walk away. Jenna & River walk up to Samuel & say thank you, Samuel says your welcome ladies then run to the garbage can on the curb to vomit in it. River & Jenna just look at each other & sigh, River saying he's our help? Jenna says he did give me permission to use him as a human shield, River rolls her big green eyes saying at least that's something. Jenna says I'll move the car looking at River tears in her eyes, they both know the only place to go at the moment is grandma's house.

Chapter 11

River opens the front door thinking of Jenna, she hasn't been here since her grandmother passed. Even sent me to get her things. River sniffles as she opens the front door, stepping inside it takes her a moment to realize everything is pristine, no smell of dust, and the furniture is wrapped in plastic, she thinks about this a moment....then it hits her & she's sobbing realizing aunt Bella did this & was keeping the house clean or paid someone too. Jenna done parking the car gets out seeing Samuel has found a place to park looks at the front door, River standing in it sobbing, she slams the car door closed & runs to her love. As she's wrapping her arms around her from behind River turns to her burying her face in her chest as Jenna holds her she looks around and sees what River has seen, & Jenna begins to cry. As the two girls are standing there holding each other & crying Samuel steps up behind them. He thinks to himself there's only one way past grief & that takes a step forward or back but it has to be taken. He does his best to be gentle then clearing his throat he gets death glares from both girls, thinking to himself don't panic, he speaks gently. I know loss as well & there's no limit to set for yourselves to grieve but remember as much as our loved ones may want to be remembered they don't want their loss to define our lives in a negative way. With nothing more he can offer them he goes silent. The two girls consider his words & Jenna says you're right thank you, Samuel, then she turns to River & says let's go to my old room, River just nods. Then Jenna says Samuel there's a guest room please, & she tears up a little sniffling she starts again. Please don't use grandma's. He nods solemnly & the two girls walk away heading upstairs. He stands there a moment realizing he doesn't know which room is which, he'll have to touch the doors & if there's enough left of their grandmother in this house he'll feel it. He walks around thinking to himself about what's happened & what's next & why Bella called him. Sure she had the authority to & regardless for her he'd still have come but he knows he's not ready for this. River & Jenna are four years younger than him & doing better without as far as he knows any training. He sighs to himself unwrapping the couch, & remembers Miss Kyle's words... this is their story they'll decide it. He thinks about it a moment, she's right & he will support them, also though whats my story?

River & Jenna use the upstairs bathroom to hold each other in the shower, Jenna thinking of something to cheer them up decides to talk about how after her grandmother passed River was at the end of the sidewalk of the school every day to walk her home, despite not wanting to be in public & how aunt Bella adopted her so the state wouldn't force her to choose a parent. Smiling through tears Jenna kept going after the other kids started picking on me...well this was the day I realized I had feelings for you River. She blushes some & says the first day you saw them following me to you, you headed right for me. River blushes & says I may have done that, smiling sheepishly. Jenna says mmhhmm. Then continued, you approached us took my hand & said, from now till always don't run. Then you faced the kids head down under your hood & said, if any of you still have your grandmother alive please go to them & tell them how you harassed Jenna about her deceased grandmother, then with a voice that made me tremble you told them, now turn around & walk away before I make it to where you never walk again. Jenna sniffles & blushes some & whispers quietly to River their faces pressed together, I fell in love with you at that moment. River smiles & kisses her. Then says let's get clean. They begin washing each other & River says Jenna I um loved you the first time you offered me a hug, I well, you know that I'd just buried my parents & other than aunt Bella no one that I remember had shown me that much kindness, I couldn't help myself Jenna, you smelled like an angels embrace & your eyes told me I'd never be alone with you by my side, of coarse those feelings have only grown stronger my love. Jenna looks at her tears streaming down her face. River says we're clean enough Jenna let's head to bed & try to sleep in the morning we should call work & then go shopping. Jenna nods & turns off the shower grabbing nothing but a hairbrush & a towel apiece they head to their bed, stopping at the bed Jenna chuckles & says I never thought we'd have to do the unwrapping of a bed, River giggles & says grab a corner you.

Lying on the couch trying to calm his mind, Samuel tries to sleep but sleep isn't coming. He keeps going over it in his mind, what's his story & why did Bella call him? He sighs thinking maybe I should call & request they send another, in The Watchers of Shadow there's no shame in admitting you need help or admitting a mission is too much for an agent. After a moment more thought he decides that's what he's gonna do, & strangely that begins to settle his mind. Starting to doze off in the silent house he hears the girls giggling. He tries to ignore them but he can't stop thinking about what they may be doing upstairs, he sighs in frustration & stands up thinking I'll just go for a walk certainly they can't go all night. As he approaches the door it hits him...go all night...even more frustrated now as his imagination of what they are doing takes over. He steps outside locking the door without thinking & closes it, takes a few steps realizing what he just did & mumbles shit! Now I'll have to sleep in my car. He decides to walk & wanders next door examining the burnt husk that had been Bella's home, after a moment he feels guilty, thinking she put her trust in me to watch over her nieces, that's the only reason to call me not someone better. He sighs & quietly thinks to her, forgive me Bella I'm a failure...but I'm going to do right by you as you did by me I'll get them a better agent & make sure they are safe. After a bit he begins to wander around the burnt house, not watching where he's going he trips over a burnt support beam falling on his face. He lays there a moment feeling stupid, when he raises his head to get up a small black cat is sitting there looking at him with an amused look on its face. Samuel says to the cat, you look amused, then he sees its eyes are just black orbs, panicking some he touches it with his power, & is happy to feel nothing negative from the cat. Samuel stands up looking down at the cat he sees white & silver spirals in its fur & the spirals are swiveling.

He rubs his eyes & thinks this is the concussion Jenna gave me & chuckles to himself over how they met. Samuel realizes then he's sweet on her, then immediately is heartbroken because he knows River has her heart. Then out of nowhere, he hears River's voice in his head soft & calming. Samuel stops hurting over Jenna, there's more than one way to win a heart & if you want her heart you need River's too. Samuel looks around surprised seeing only the little black cat he realizes River referred to herself in the third person. He laughs out loud, it's the concussion he says looking at the little black cat. They look at each other quietly, the cat still looking amused. Finally, Samuel says good night little kitty thanks for the company. Samuel walks over to his car to get in still thinking in the morning make the call it's the right thing, when he reaches the car the little black cat is sitting on the sidewalk by the driver's side door. Samuel touches the cat again searching for anything with his mind, but nothing it's just a cat. Speaking out loud Samuel says to the cat, little guy I'm sorry I've got nothing for you please run home. Waiting as if the cat is going to respond in some way Samuel decides he's just going to open the door & step over it. Reaching for the car door the cat jumps at him hitting him in the chest then runs off. Samuel shakes his head & gets in the car. Driver seat reclined he thinks to himself maybe one more try before I fall asleep, reaching in his coat pocket he searches for Bella's picture...wait he thinks sitting up. He opens his coat & looks down at the inside breast pocket where he carried the three pictures, the pocket is empty & it's unzipped. Samuel thinks about it & remembers zipping it back up after showing the girls their pictures since Jenna took them, so how? He leans back thinking about this, obviously, the cat couldn't have done this, he thinks about all his interactions today, the girls….no neither one of them got within arms reach of him….the police officer, mmm maybe he thinks but not likely. Samuel falls asleep thinking about it & other impossible things.

Before the girls sleep Jenna looks at River snuggled against her face to face, & says I can't stop thinking about the last time we were with grandma, River kisses her gently & says I'm thinking about it too. They both remember the day she died sitting on either side of her she hadn't gotten out of bed that morning, and the nurse called them into the room. They sat on either side of her holding her hands. Both looking at each other trying not to cry. River looked around the room some trying to memorize it, pictures of family everywhere. The one she liked the most was of Jenna & her parents taken sometime before they divorced, all three smiling and looking so happy. River smiles just a little selfishly thinking to herself Jenna smiles like that for me. Then their grandmother moved their hands together she didn't know she had woken up. Putting River's & Jenna's hands together she said, forever & always you two. After that, she fell asleep & never woke up again. Jenna asks River, do you think she knew River? River smiles through tears & says I like to think so. Both girls with happy tears fall asleep. In the morning the girls relieve themselves & shower. When they call their boss there's no surprise she already knows being in such a small town, all their boss says is whenever you two are ready come back, take all the time you need. After the phone call they go downstairs & see the couch is unwrapped,

Jenna says, maybe I should have shown him the guest room, River says, only maybe. Both girls giggling go outside River keeping her hood on of course looks towards her aunt's home & says out loud, good bye aunt Bella love you. Jenna hugs her & says look, he actually slept in his car! River laughs a little & asks do you know anything about men? Jenna says no, I didn't even date a boy at school, do you River? River looks at her a moment then says, these eyes are only for you my love. Jenna smiles big & blushes sighing she says, I don't believe either of us are missing anything. After that, they do their shopping stop by the park for a little bit feeding the ducks then head home. When they get there they see Samuel still asleep in his car, River jokes & says let's get him a bumper sticker saying warning: guard on duty, they both laugh going inside. They stop at the door look at each other & decide to leave it unlocked for Samuel, because despite all their teasing they are glad to have him, he's kind to them & has helped them quite a bit, also Bella chose him. Walking to the kitchen the girls laugh agreeing to keep him. They get the food put away & pull out what they want to eat. Jenna wants hard-boiled eggs, some bacon & toast. River tells her make enough eggs for me please I'll put it in my tuna. Jenna just chuckles at her but of course throws an extra for her in the pot. They even make sure to make enough for Samuel. While peeling the eggs Samuel finally comes in, following his nose, he goes to the kitchen standing at the door he politely says hello ladies, they turn & say hello back & River says breakfast will be ready soon Samuel if you want, you have time for a quick shower. Samuel says thank you, then adds I love the smell of tuna & eggs in the morning! Both girls grab an unpeeled egg & throw it at him hitting him in the head, then River reaches back grabs the butter she was going to put on her toasted tuna sandwich throws it at him as he's recovering, hitting him in the mouth saying here! Put a stick-o-butter on it! Then the girls turn back & finish peeling eggs. Samuel confused at least picks up the eggs & butter reaching as far as he can putting them on the end of the counter & fleeing the kitchen. On his way to the bathroom to clean up Samuel thinks about what just happened, it takes him a moment then he realizes, tuna describes...well um a feminine smell. Shit! He thinks to himself eggs? Oh fuck! How do I apologize? Thinking this over he cleans up and then realizes I just need to go call, once they have a better-suited agent here for them I'll have apologized enough. He wipes his face & goes to use the phone he saw in the front room. While he's talking to his superior filling him in Jenna & River decide to go find Samuel together & tell him breakfast is ready & try not to mention tuna & egg smells in the morning. They hear him on the phone talking...yes director I'm sure, I am NOT qualified for this mission I will stay until a more qualified agent arrives & fill him or her in on the situation & you in person sir as this information is to sensitive to relay over the phone. The girls can't hear the person on the other end, but looking at each other they see that both of them disagree with Samuel's choice. Then they hear Samuel say, yes sir thank you, sir. Samuel hangs up the phone & sighs rubbing his face with his left hand. From behind him, he hears Jenna say, I should have kicked his fucking head off. Tone flat & harsh he stiffens then slowly turns around. River & Jenna death glaring at him. Samuel holds up his right hand motioning them to wait & says please let me explain. River immediately says, can't wait to hear this shit! Samuel looks hurt but speaks up, I'm very sorry River & Jenna but as we all know I cannot fulfill my duty, you both need someone better equipped to handle what is coming, they are sending agent Alexis Anora, don't worry she's fought shadows before & shes good with um...females, the last part he said quietly. Jenna speaks up first, you mean to say she has a spine & has combat experience & a vagina. Samuel looking all embarrassed tries to speak but River cuts him off saying, I bet agent vagina never ran out on a mission or let Aunt Bella down or her two nieces for that matter! Before he can say anything Jenna says, it was about six hours he told me that he had talked to Aunt Bella last before teleporting me, I bet River, we have time to eat pack & head to Portland before agent vagina gets hers. River looks at Jenna & says let's do it love, & without looking at Samuel they go back to the kitchen to eat breakfast. Samuel standing there thinking about this does see the girl's perspective, but decides he's right telling himself, I'm older & more experienced. He sighs & besides he chokes up some, & thinks if you two die under another agent's watch I won't have lost what's left of Bella myself. Samuel just stands there not knowing how long, when River & Jenna come marching in, bags over both shoulders, they stop in front of him, then River says, Samuel, we want you to know we understand your situation some, your afraid of failing & you don't know how to talk to us. Jenna says then, Samuel, we are grateful to you for saving my life & for all the help you've given us but we are not accepting help from anyone Aunt Bella didn't recommend. Jenna goes quiet looking at River, River continues, by saying Aunt Bella emphasizing aunt, which means not our mom, do you know about my mother? Her name was Willow Fey. He looks up & shakes his head, River says we don't either but Aunt Bella said she had been a problem, we trusted Aunt Bella, River stops there looking at Jenna. I'm done Jenna says quietly, the girls both hug him a moment then say you know where we're going if you change your mind, Samuel. The girls leave Samuel just standing there fighting guilt & to his surprise grief, he hears the trunk of the car close wincing a little, then two car doors, and shortly after the motor turns over & idling. Then as he hears the car pulling away he screams out loud in frustration, he stands there a bit not sure what to do, and then he feels a presence activate his power & he looks around. Sitting in the recliner still covered in plastic sits a figure he doesn't recognize, glowing with a blueish light. Beside it on the couch a younger River, he hears an old lady's voice asking do you love my Jenna & a young River blushes saying yes I do. Then he hears the old lady say I'm glad River you'll always fill each other's hearts. Tears running down Samuel's face he knows somewhat of what he's seeing, though never this vivid before, it's a memory with great power or it would have faded from this house already, but why is he seeing it now? As the two energies fade he hears what he can only describe as a sword striking a shield. Now more confused than ever he just shrugs helplessly not knowing what to do. As he stands there he hears River's soft voice in his head again: it's not too late Samuel, & they do need your help. He stiffens, mind searching he feels the small black cat, Samuel looks around & when he looks through the door to the kitchen it's sitting on the table helping itself to the tuna left out as he watches he chokes up a little thinking probably left for me, then laughs out loud hearing: here! Put a stick-o-butter on it! He decides right there that he's going to help them, putting all his doubts aside, realizing to himself, this is my story! He walks over to the table petting the cat, it looks up at him & begins to purr. Samuel says thank you & in his head softly in River's voice he hears: always & forever. He chokes up remembering that's what River had said to Jenna when they found her in the bathroom. Thinking to himself about last night he recalls, there's more than one way to win a heart. He realizes love is many things, going to the phone he calls his superior, and when they answer he says, something has changed, before they can ask what he says, I have new information about two agents that I know is not on record, also River & Jenna will not accept another agent. His superior asks him how do you know this? Samuel says, not on an unsecured line sir, but I can say this, if another agent is sent to watch over River & Jenna we will lose them. The superior says who will we lose? Samuel says, everything. Then says, staying on this assignment & without waiting for permission or confirmation hangs up & heads for the door, this time locking it on purpose.

Chapter 12

Sitting in an air-conditioned office in Indiana the director hangs up the phone drumming the fingers of his left hand on his desk. Looking at the blank white walls as he does, Samuel Nigeus is young only his second mission….he could be in trouble. Thinking some more he does know Bella is one of the best agents to ever walk the fabled halls of The Watchers of Shadow, even saved his life. Looking at the plague on the wall running his fingers through his grey beard, he reads Semper Fi, that's enough for him. He picks up the phone dialing his assistant, when he answers he says, Jonathan tell Alexis Anora to see me before she leaves for Oregon, Jonathan just says yes Director. The old Director hangs up his phone & leans back waiting & thinks to himself what did he mean by "everything". His mind goes back to the day Bella saved him. He was bleeding out & with the loss of blood, he knew everything he'd seen wasn't necessarily what happened. Pinned down, fellow agents dead he was hiding a child from a cult & they were coming. The cult members entered the room he was in & he knew this was it checking his mp5 he was ready, the child under the floorboards below his feet. The wall exploded in front of him & he heard men & women screaming, he was confused for a moment then thought it must be the backup he'd requested. While listening to the screams trying not to black out from loss of blood she was just there, like she materialized. A sword in her right hand, in his bloodlossed state he figured he'd hallucinated all this because the sword moved as though it was fluid. Either way, Bella saved his life & that child's that's all he needed to know. Finally, there's a knock at the door he says enter. Opening the door & entering is Alexis Anora, five foot eight, with short blonde hair & brown eyes, she looks like any other woman who could be anywhere from 20 to 30. She steps forward as he stands up & says yes Director? He says hello Alexis, the director calling her by her first name immediately knows this is not an official meeting knowing her uncle as she does. So she asks, what's up Uncle Jim? He says I'm not sure but...he tells her about Samuel's mission & Samuel, ending with all he knows of Bella. Alexis says this sounds like a bad situation, is this Samuel Nigeus believable? The director says unknown but he too knows Bella. Taking in a breath he says do this right Alexis, assume at the moment Samuel is right, so cryptic communication when you check in, & observe from afar. Once you know enough of what's going on coordinate with me if possible, but use your best judgment. Alexis nods & says yes uncle. She leaves, heading to Wheeler

boarding a private plane to review her brief, since it's the last known contact for agent Nigeus & the two girls in his protection. Upon arriving she sees that the house at the address has burned to the ground. She stops at the curb leaving her suburban running & walks over to examine the burned-down house, her abilities tell her the fire that did this wasn't of natural origins. She tries for more but doesn't get anything, kneeling running her fingers over a burned piece of wood she hears a single thought in her head, in a soft female voice she hears, right! She immediately looks right & all she sees is a house next door in the backyard a gazebo is partially in view. Looking around for a moment she sees nothing but decides to walk over to the house that is in the direction of the voice, as she approaches her instincts scream, being hunted! She reaches for her pistol, a .45 caliber acp with 285 grain hollow points as she's learned overkill is the only option as an agent of Watchers of Shadow. As she approaches the house she hugs the wall & moves to a window looking through all she sees is a curtain, mentally sighing still feeling hunted she moves to the backyard, which has an eight-foot-tall privacy fence of course. She takes a moment to focus then reaches up with her left hand grips the top of the fence as good as possible & leaps the fence, using her left hand to guide her. Hitting the grass-covered ground on the other side her instincts immediately tell her this was a very, very bad idea. Suddenly her peripheral vision picks up a blur on her right immediately she rolls back hearing claws just missing her head, coming up on one knee gun at the ready, there's nothing. Then she's wrapped from behind, she doesn't even look just puts her pistol beside her head & fires, her hearing protection barely holds out. She hears a roar but can move rolling forward she turns to see a shadow but with a humanoid face & tentacles where the lips should be. Saving her own life Alexis doesn't hesitate & unloads the last eleven 285-grain hollow points into the shadow's face. Stunned it's still standing she knows retreat is the only option, as she turns she drops the spent clip & reloads lightning fast, even tucking the spent clip in her pocket. Taking four long strides she leaps the privacy fence & runs around the house to her suburban, opening the back door she grabs a full auto combat shotgun loaded with phosphorus rounds & steps around the side of the suburban waiting. But nothing happens, cautiously Alexis returns to check the backyard & house finding only a bowl licked clean on the table, and the unwrapped bed & couch. Alexis is not sure how to proceed, so she goes to her suburban & puts her shotgun away & sits in the driver's seat reloads her spent clip listening to the police scanner. She hears an odd conversation, a policewoman speaking into the radio says, just seen the red Mercedes Benz, with the two females inside looks like they took the on-ramp towards Portland, followed by a black Ford Mercury. Alexis listens as she knows those cars from her report. She hears another voice firm & a little angry respond on the radio, I will not say this again! There is no protocol to survey those three civilians, For some reason the voice emphasized civilians, and then she hears stand down that's an order! Alexis already started driving looking for the freeway knowing, that's agent Samuel Nigeus & the girls River Fey & Jenna Vella. She thinks Lucky Me small-town cops for not knowing how to speak on a radio & yes it seems Agent Samuel was correct.

Nullsoul, takes the portal opened by The Unseen Ones into the Shadow Girls realm, materializing he's ready to faze. He's in a small thicket of trees, he listens & expands his senses it's night & he hears an owl in the distance. It doesn't take him long to realize his targets are close. He moves fazed not completely in this realm, as he approaches the area he can sense his targets and he realizes The Unseen Ones got him close, he sees the burned structure where fought his last target, still knowing he didn't kill his prey that day he's alert not knowing if it has returned. Watching the structure beside it he feels his prey inside as he moves closer. Cautiously, remembered his last encounter with them & how he'd underestimated them. Not again he thinks, right now his tactic or plan is separate them eliminating them one at a time. As he watches he sees a male leaving the structure & thinks to himself that this may be an ally, & it's alone so he'll eliminate it given the chance. Watching it he's confused, the prey stops a few steps away from the structure looks back then stomps its foot & shakes its hands. Nullsoul wonders if something is wrong with this one. As he watches he sees the prey moving toward the burned structure, isolated & alone he moves closer. Watching the prey it moves around the structure, not seeing the object on the ground it falls over it not even being able to prevent its fall the prey is on the ground face down. Nullsoul actually sighs to himself pondering the prey, at this point he thinks killing it may actually aid the Shadow Girl. Finally, Nullsoul thinks to himself nonetheless if it's an ally I have orders. Before Nullsoul can faze fully into the realm the small black cat is there in front of the prey. Nullsoul immediately withdraws, once he feels safe he snarls at his weakness, fear made him withdraw nothing else. As he continues Watching he realizes there is no chance to take this prey at the moment, the small black cat is interacting with it, he decides to wait until the small black cat is nowhere to be seen. Nullsoul waits until morning & the two female prey are leaving. He thinks about his options, stalk those two or stay & try to eliminate the prey that seems damaged. Nullsoul decides to stay. Once the two females are gone he approaches the prey, then stops as he sees the little black cat circling one of the round objects holding up the small structure the prey is in, this time snarling to himself he refuses to retreat but does not engage either, so he continues to wait. It's some time but he finally sees his opportunity, the females leave & the male is in the structure alone. Nullsoul circles around to the back moving through the privacy fence, once inside he stops. Something is wrong, not sure what it is he searches using all his senses...suddenly he hears something close to his head moving to avoid....nothing? He looks around, there's nothing! Nullsoul not happy with this takes a step toward the structure & he smells the scent of the prey he knows he didn't kill, immediately he moves circling the interior of the fence, then looks at what he sees as a structure with no walls is his prey, the one he lost. The prey is fighting another, female with a sword & some other object he doesn't recognize attached to her left arm using it to deflect the sword of the other. Nullsoul watches them & realizes they aren't fighting not really, they have looks of enjoyment on their faces & appear to be laughing at times. Confused Nullsoul watches this & time goes by, he doesn't even realize his prey has left or that the little black cat is watching amused. Then Nullsoul hearing a sound to his left snaps out of...whatever was happening to him & sees a new female he doesn't recognize, crouched on the ground holding something in her hand he also doesn't recognize. Immediately Nullsoul moves to kill this new prey. Aiming for its head he moves swiping with his left arm claws extended....miss?

How? He fazes getting behind his prey and grabbing her. He sees a flash of movement, fire then pain. His ears rang, as he locked eyes on his prey it pointed the object at him he didn't recognize, then there were several loud noises fire coming from the end of it & pain so much burning pain! Through one eye lightening fast he sees the prey spin its hands moving doing something with the painful object it's holding then after four steps it jumps the wood standing on the ground, he moves to pursue it but stops checking himself, disappointed realizing he should feed before engaging the new prey, fazing & roaring in frustration he goes to hunt....the little black cat looking out of the rear kitchen window still on the table has a content look on its face.

Chapter 13

River & Jenna leave not sure if they are upset at Samuel or just upset that they may have just lost someone else. Pulling up to the gas station River takes a deep breath pulls up her hood & says I'll get gas you grab us a road map. Jenna looks at her clearly showing concern, River kisses her & says I'll be ok love it's just our first real road trip together, Jenna smiles and touches River's cheek with her fingertips just looking at her. Then says ok River be right back. The girls get out River gets the gas & Jenna sprints inside the store, grabbing a road map, as she gets in line she sighs, it's a small town & the old man must know the attendant because they are talking about getting together for something this weekend. She's not tall enough to look over the raised counter through the window at five foot six inches to check on River, so she just fidgets waiting. After a bit she looks up & says excuse me, nothing happens, so she reaches around the old man in front of her slightly stepping left & places the road map & a five-dollar bill on the counter. The attendant sees her do this & goes back to his conversation. Jenna gets pissed, grabs the map leaves the money & starts walking out as she does the attendant says hey you didn't pay for that, as she turns the old man sees her, a sad look forming on his face, he turns to the attendant & says yes she did. The attendant tries to open his mouth but the old man just says have a nice day Jenna, surprised since she doesn't recognize the old man just smiles politely & says thank you. Getting back to the car she gets in putting her hand on River's thigh & says I'm sorry are you ok? River smiles starting the car & says yes Jenna, as they are leaving Jenna clips her seatbelt & tells River what happened & that she didn't know the old man. River says probably one of Grandma's friends or maybe Aunt Bella's, remember small town. Jenna says, your right, thinking a moment then adds going to miss it. River looks at her & says we'll come home again love. Looking at the road map Jenna tries to remember when she started calling Bella aunt & River calling Jenna's grandmother grandma & laughing to herself realizing she doesn't know but it doesn't matter they are family. After a bit Jenna writes down instructions from the map & shows River, saying it's basically a straight line, eighty-five miles roughly, River takes a deep breath & says I've never driven seventy-five for that long, Jenna says you got this River besides I haven't either, yawning she tries to stay awake, River watches her & yes she nervous but tells her to take a nap Jenna. Jenna looks at her questioning but River insists so Jenna curls up in the seat her head on River's right thigh, nervously River reaches down with her right hand using her fingertips to stroke Jenna's hair, it works in a few minutes she's asleep River smiling to herself. Jenna finds herself standing outside Aunt Bella's house seeing it as it used to look, thinking to herself that's not right, then remembers my heads in River's lap sleeping I have to be dreaming. As she watches the house burst into flames she ducks putting her hands over her face, and then realizes she can't feel the heat of the flame or smell smoke. She relaxes & looks around she sees her grandmother's house & four others on the street then there's forest all around, she notices it's night or seems to be looking at the sky she doesn't see a moon or stars, it's just black. She sighs & looks back to Bella's house the fire is out not even smoke. Standing there she thinks to herself, this has to be the slowest dream ever, usually, River is in her dreams sometimes she dreams of work, and she even dreams of school still sometimes even though she graduated over four months ago. Thinking some more she realizes this dream seems very real, she calls out hello, helloooooo! Then she hears River's voice, no need to yell beautiful I hear you, looking around excited River is here she sees a small black cat, recognizing River's description she sees dark eyes & silver white spirals in its fur she hesitates a little as the small black cat sits at her feet looking up amused. Jenna takes a small step back looks down takes a deep breath calming herself then says um…hello there. The cat using River's voice says & hello to you too, I'm glad you're taking this well even though we are here & time flows slower it still flows & you will have to wake up soon. Jenna kneels looking the cat in the eye & says you're not here to hurt us, are you? The small cat looks amused & just says perspectives, Jenna, then it stands up & says follow me please & walks around the burnt house, Jenna not knowing what else to do follows. On the way she asks, are you Odiewan that Aunt Bella described? The cat getting to where it's going stops turns around twice then sits down & looks up at her amused look on its face again. The cat is quiet a moment & says, for my old friend yes I was Odiewan, for you & River maybe not you two will decide. Jenna kneels reaching out & asks may I? The cat gets up running its head under her hand and going down its back Jenna smiles & pets the cat it purs for her. Jenna asks why do you use River's voice? The cat getting a good petting & purring asks why do you use Jenna's voice? Jenna remembering what her aunt said about Odiewan answering in riddles takes a deep breath eyes widening understanding something. The cat sits looking up at her & says my apologies Jenna but we can take no more time at this time to build our friendship. Then ask do you feel that? Jenna looks at him she does feel something, she nods & says what is it? The cat looks towards the burnt house still sitting he says a gift, a sacrifice. Then the burnt rubble is gone & all that's left is the foundation of the house. The cat looks at Jenna & says to do or don't doesn't matter, you have proven your love to River. She looks at the cat confused & asks are you questioning my love for River? The cat answers her directly for the first time saying there's nothing in this realm or any other that can question your love for River, adding brighter than all the moon & stars. Jenna smiles saying thank you. The cat says take your gift or not but the time of choosing this day has come. Looking towards the foundation Jenna decides to look because Odiewan is not her enemy & aunt Bella trusted him she gets up & walks over looking down feeling a slight pull on her she sees a sword lying on the concrete floor of the basement. Remembering Aunt Bella saying, "I'm Valkyrie, no shield no fear" she realizes what this must be. How...she's not so sure. She feels what she must do if she's taking the gift she reaches her right hand out tearing up, sighing sacrifice. The sword moves incredibly fast straight to her hand, she has time to feel the grip before she hears River scream, Jenna! Wake the fuck up!

After a bit River begins to relax, seventy-five isn't so bad in a 99 Mercedes Benz, the car Aunt Bella bought her after she got her driver's license. As the other drivers don't bother her now they just go around her & when need be she goes around them. She plays her & Jenna's favorite song, and as she's singing I'd do anything she feels it thinking cathululips! She looks just in time to see him swing & miss in the rearview immediately her foot buries the gas pedal in the floorboard screaming Jenna! Wake the fuck up!

As Samuel pulls into the gas station just before the freeway entrance he sees the girl's car heading up the on-ramp & thinks I'm coming I refuse to fail. Filling his car he realizes he's starving thinking to himself gastation food he heads in. He hears an old man going off on a shamed-looking attendant while he grabs some snacks & bottled water, seeing the case of black tea next to it he thinks of the girls & decides it may help me apologize remembering the hurt look in their eyes. He walks up to the counter he hears the old man finish his lecture, you never know what's happening to people that you interact with, & if I EVER find out your pocketing money from the customers again I'll tell your sister & within two hours all of Wheeler will know. The attendant pissed his pants, Samuel smiled to himself as the old man turns & says my apologies sir, seeing Samuel's smile he asks is this funny to you? Samuel says, yes sir but only because I just got a similar lecture but from two sixteen-year-old girls & if it takes the rest of my life I will apologize to them. The old man eyes Samuel a moment then looks at the attendant & says learn from him, boy! Samuel places his snacks water & the girl's tea on the counter pays thanks the attendant & nods sir to the old man & heads out. Later he's doing ninety trying to catch up to the girls. When he finally sees their car he breathes a sigh of relief for just a second, then he sees a shadow appear next to their car claw swiping, it misses & then he figures whoever is driving panicked because the car lurches & accelerates & he knows his ford won't keep up with the Mercedes but he tries anyway.

Alexis not needing fuel & having energy bars sees the Ford on the on-ramp as she passes the gas station happy she's on the right track hits the freeway. Samuel must be in a hurry she thinks he's speeding. Sloppy she thinks or desperate because he just risks a highway patrolman pulling him over. As she's driving she thinks just an hour & ten minutes roughly but I should catch up if I don't I'll lose them in Portland. Slightly annoyed she speeds up hoping the suburban will keep up with their cars. As she's speeding Alexis sees she's keeping up & is relieved it will make it easier. Then from where she is on the freeway she sees the shadow she fought before swiping at the car, seeing the car speed up & the shadow behind them, she says " You're not faster than a car I may not have recognized you completely but you're still a shadow. Then disbelief as it teleports ahead of the car almost beyond even her range of sight. Fuck! She thinks to herself what have the three of them got hunting them? Seeing the car stop she immediately puts the suburban on the shoulder of the freeway looking forward checking the situation, the shadow caught & threw a car at their car, it missed the car he threw smashing into the front end of Samuel's Ford. Alexis knowing a little about this shadow from her first encounter says to herself, no such thing as overkill. Climbing in the back seat she opens a large rifle case smiling pulling out the 50 cal. Thinking finally! She climbs out into the dirt & then jumps onto the top of the suburban turning and facing the others half a mile away, she deploys the barrel stands on the 50 cal. Snugging the butt to her right shoulder she calms her breathing looking through the scope seeing everything & confirms...hello there tentacle lips. She has the shot just as something moves in the line. Thinking to herself is that River?

Nullsoul finds prey quickly & feeds killing a small family of three. He growls a little thinking even weak it shouldn't have taken three of these weaklings. Then he hears The Unseen Ones in his head just one word. Learn. He thinks about this & agrees, the one that did this was far too fast to be one of the weak ones of this realm also it's weapon even if it's not the most powerful in its arsenal he can't take it for long. Keeping this in mind as well he picks up their scent & teleports. He's at some sort of structure an acrid smell in the air as well that he doesn't recognize but he recognizes the prey, searching some he follows their scent it only takes a moment & he sees the prey their black structure moving faster heading away from him. He pursues trying to catch them, believing they are at a disadvantage in their small structure moving as fast as they are. He will have to use the barriers to teleport & put himself in the right place. Trying several times he's met with frustration, either too far ahead & his prey will be alerted, or too far away to act. Also even not fully in their realm, something happens when the metal structures pass through him & it disorientates him for several seconds. Nullsoul focuses he believes he's the greatest hunter, I will catch them he says to himself. Finally, he teleports & is next to them seeing the Shadow Girl controlling the metal structure moving her mouth tapping on some round object in one hand & excited seeing the mate sleeping in her lap. Feeling confident he's caught them off guard he fully fazes into their realm swiping, claws extended at the car. He misses, angry he moves into the lane the metal object moving much faster now he growls in rage as he knows the Shadow Girl senses him, he thinks for a split second she's fleeing I still have the advantage. He decides to try something, he teleports aiming for just ahead of them. He overcaculated & was further ahead than he wanted seeing a metal structure heading straight at him it slid making noise, the small round structures on the bottom not turning. It stops & Nullsoul steps up to it grabbing it burying his claws in it picking it up he throws it at his prey. Their structure passes under it missing. As he begins to anger seeing it hit the structure behind it he sees that one had prey in it as well. Good that one I will still be able to kill, then the Shadow Girl's black structure stops in front of him & the prey steps out. This time he sees the difference in his prey, its eyes are glowing green, blue outlined purple energy swarming through her. Having already been beaten by this prey once, very badly, he feels fear. Roaring out loud he thinks to himself noooo! I will destroy this prey! It's this preys fault I was banished & fed on....it will know my hatred....

Chapter 14

Jenna hearing River telling her to wake up immediately responds no time to think she's disorientated, then River's right arm pins her to the seat & she feels the car coming to a stop she hears their favorite song playing. Before she can enjoy it River puts the car in park & steps out. Jenna seeing her power lighting up her skin is stunned for a moment then looks out the windshield and sees Cathululips. In her head she hears River's voice, no one can question your love for River. Sniffling she climbs out the driver's side hearing Cathululips roar. She's scared possibly peed a little as she steps up beside River. River doesn't even look at her & without any emotion says, help Samuel & she's gone, Jenna turns her head in time to see her blast into Cathululips smiling to herself she thinks ya....ya River's got this & looks thinking... help Samuel? Looking back she sees his car crushed under another & she says figures wed end up taking care of him. Truly worried though she runs to him, when she gets there he's kicking at the door. Without thinking Jenna grabs the door & yanks it off the car. Standing up she looked down in her hands was the car door, also she'd squeezed it so hard her fingers were buried in the fiberglass. Samuel free now stands up next to her a confused look on his face, looking between her & the car door. Finally, he says thank you, Jenna. She looks up at him & shrugs tosses the car door aside & says with a giant proud smile, River's kicking Cathululips ass! They turn to watch & Samuel sees Cathululips he screams at such a pitch he sounds like a girl. Jenna sticking one finger in her ear looks at him & says bitch much? He looks embarrassed not answering.

Alexis watching thinks to herself move girl! I've got this! Then River does move, so quickly she misses it & smashes into tentacle lips. Alexis watches stunned not knowing what to do now, then seeing the blonde girl, she reminds herself, Jenna yes Jenna, rip the driver's side door of Samuel's car. For the first time in a long time of being an agent, she's speechless. Alexis refocuses watching tentacle lips.

River smashes into Cathululips, not all rage but not knowing much about fighting lets her power do the work. It works for a moment smashing his face in she doesn't hesitate she throws her punches fast & hard breaking him quickly. She's even faster than him. Dodging his blows easily.

Nullsoul stands his ground as The Shadow Girl charges him thinking I'm the more skilled you are nothing. When the prey hits him he realizes he's not faster than it & must use his skill. He strikes out using his feet & hands. The prey keeps moving! I can't hit it, and then he feels something break inside him, whatever she broke he struggles to breathe. Noooo!! He shouts into his mind, I will not lose again! Teleporting behind her he grabs her, thinking now!

As Cathululips teleports behind River she hesitates a moment thinking just like before....wait he grabs her from behind. In this state River is all focus so she doesn't panic but has to think of something, realizing she needs to learn how to fight. Then she hears her voice in her head again... Shadows are your playthings remember? Then she reaches out not with her hands but with her energy. What few shadows are cast in the mid-morning sun begin to darken & grow. Her shadow, Cathululips's shadow, Mercedes's shadow even Samuel's & Jenna's. River feels what she's doing & knows she's got this. Before she can do anything with it she hears zzzziiippp & a thud followed by an extremely loud crack! Almost explosive. Cathululips disappears.

Watching River & Tentacle lips engage each other Alexis is mystified in all her years as an agent & listening to her uncle Jim's stories she has never seen anything like this before or heard of it. River is faster than her eye can see & from what she can tell stronger than anything she's ever heard of watching this she thinks this girls got this. So she continues watching. When Tentacle lips disappears she has time to barely think she made him retreat...then he's behind her holding her, Alexis gets ready, he's taller, and I see her feet on the ground....headshot. Then she sees the shadows growing bigger and darker & she immediately thinks his power! Alexis squeezes the trigger thinking she's saving River. This time when he vanishes she believes he's dead. No way he survived the 50. She watches a moment, Jenna running up to River hugging her giving her...Alexis smiles seeing them kissing & thinks that's love. She surveys the area seeing it's clear & no immediate threats except the sounds of approaching authorities she steps off the suburban puts the rifle in its case slamming the top closed letting the quick locks do the rest & drives up to talk to Samuel.

Jenna runs to River & hugs her kisses her softly & says from now until forever. River smiles & says from now until forever my sweet Jenna. Then River says, I can beat him, I can kill Cathululips. Jenna smiles & says I know you can. They look at each other for a moment just enjoying they are alive & together then River's face gets serious, at first Jenna thinks it's about her. But River turns keeping her hand in Jenna's & says Samuel! Samuel stiffens thinking what did I do? River tugging Jenna with her storms up to him. Taking a breath she says thank you politely & softly Samuel relaxes a bit & says my pleasure River, before he can enjoy her gratitude any further she says, next time do NOT shoot him I had that. He looks confused, & says I didn't though. River says then who? Jenna even says, he didn't River I was standing next to him the whole time, all he did was bitch scream. Then River & Jenna see the suburban pulling up having made its way through the stopped traffic & River & Jenna say together, time to go. Samuel looking through the windshield of the suburban doesn't recognize the driver. As she gets out she yells wait at the girls who because of his hesitation left Samuel standing there. River looks back at her & says I will say this once...leave us alone, leave & do not look back. Then Jenna says, Samuel come! As Samuel turns to get in the car Alexis pulls out her credentials, seeing her reach behind herself Samuel responds with all his speed pistol out & points at her face. Alexis says, easy agent Samuel Nigeus, just getting my credentials so we can be properly introduced...very quick hands by the way she adds a little smile on her face. She slowly brings her credentials out holding them up for Samuel noting his eyes didn't even look at them, he says my apologies agent Anora, & lowers his gun looks past her seeing the emergency vehicles coming looks at River & says go if we get separated I can find you if you stay with your car. River just says whatever & gets in Jenna standing on the passenger side running board says Samuel! He looks around at her, she asks why are you ditching us for agent vagina? River's giggled, looking to her left out the window and listening. Before Samuel responds, Alexis asks agent vagina? Samuel looks back blushing Jenna content gets in closing the door as River is already leaving he says I'll explain later agent Anora, she knows he's being teased for something by two teenage girls so she smiles sweetly as she's getting in & says you'd better agent penis.

Nullsoul is lying in the chamber of The Unseen Ones dying. Even for The Shadow Hunter, he's taken too much damage & even if somehow he were conscious he wouldn't be able to feed. The Unseen Ones contemplate what to do with him. Discussing what has transpired they come to a decision. Nullsoul is outnumbered & they do not know what the golden-haired female is but they know that the two Watchers of Shadow are predestined & blessed. As for The Shadow Girl, they cannot determine. So The Unseen Ones knowing loyalty or not from Nullsouls actions his hatred for

The Shadow Girl will be enough drive to keep him fighting. So they revive him & give him a new edge. Once conscious Nullsoul knows where he is & readies himself for pain. Deserved or not he expects to be punished, after a time nothing happens so he remains on bended knee waiting. As he waits he feels something inside him changing, as it develops he feels his mind-expanding & feels new power within. When he feels the changing stop he hears The Unseen Ones…Nullsoul you have proven your loyalty this day, you have also learned, this day, so we will pity you. Thinking to himself pity me? He's disgusted he feels grudgingly admitting to himself to a superior predator, even in his hatred he can accept this. The Unseen Ones continue, Nullsoul take our gift & put it to good use, you will have a chance soon to strike at those who struck you down from behind, take your vengeance kill these two & the Shadow Girl & her mate will have no more allies. Hearing this Nullsoul is renewed not knowing it wasn't the Shadow Girl that defeated him. With hatred coating his words like venom he replies, with pleasure masters! He's teleported back to the Shadow Girls realm, he's inside a dark structure, and memories from his childhood return in a flash. Chained to a wall in a stone room a woman wearing white clothes tells him he's the future of The Watchers of Shadow, he still doesn't know what she meant but again he asks why am I kept here & all the women ever says is for your safety my child. Nullsoul remembers that is all she ever called him, looking up at her seeing gold hair tied tightly behind her head, and blue eyes, he feels his anger rising as it reminds him of The Shadow Girls mate, you will know pain I will not feed on your mate, I will let you watch me remove her innards slowly as she calls to you for help! He swears to himself. As the memories fade he fazes & leaves the structure, & finds their scent, The Unseen Ones putting them in their path again! This time the defective male & the new female are together in a moving structure. He follows them. Waiting patiently he sees them stop at a structure that smells acrid like the first one he'd tracked them to, this one much larger & with more of them. He watches the two speaking at each other in the moving structure as he does he unintentionally starts to feel some of the minds around him, the innermost thoughts.... their dread! This is what The Unseen Ones meant by improving him! If he can cause dread in even a few of these creatures he can feed while in combat. He calms himself to do so now would only attract attention & alert the prey...he waits. Finally the defective one & the new female get out of the structure, and to his joy, the defective one moves to the larger structure, he follows. Once inside he sees the defective one moving to the back of the structure, recognizing the drawings on the wall Nullsoul knows he's going to be in a room with only the entrance as the exit & alone. Nullsoul follows. Once inside he sees him leaking fluids into some kind of container on the wall & thinks in a moment defective one you will no longer be defective. Nullsoul moves into the realm thinking of just taking it from behind as he approaches the defective one lifts its head & Nullsoul notices a change in its posture. As he hears a sound from in front of the defective one he doesn't recognize he feels some power emanating from it Nullsoul hesitates in surprise thinking the defective one has power? Then the prey turned fast for its kind a weapon in its hand, Nullsoul recognized it as one of the things that hurt him, to late as the prey let out a high-pitched scream it uses its weapon, Nullsoul covers his face as that's where the pain is realizing this weapon doesn't hurt as much as the last one when the pain stops Nullsoul moves striking just the structure, confused he searches & the prey is outside the structure... how! Nullsoul thinks then teleports himself. Once outside near the prey, he sees the new female weapon in hand, Nullsoul knows to avoid this one & teleports behind her burying the claws of his right hand deep into her lower back he lifts her off her feet looking at the defective one roaring. He rushes the defective one feeling most of the creatures around him panicking two of them with dread & he's glad knowing if he actually needs to feed he can. Closing the distance in a heartbeat to the defective one it lets out the high-pitched scream using its weapon again. As Nullsoul towers over his prey the one on his right claw turns to him looking him in the eye. How the prey did this Nullsoul could not fathom, looking him in the eye he did not see the female's weapon come up under his chin, but he felt it. Nullsoul is hurt badly again he uses his new power to feed immediately healed....his prey has vanished! Both of them! He roars in anger standing there a moment waiting for a portal from The Unseen Ones to punish him on his return but it does not come, instead more of the creatures appear pointing their weapons at him. Nullsoul doesn't wait since they are not prey he fazes & resumes the hunt for his prey.

Chapter 15

Samuel & Alexis follow River & Jenna. Samuel still blushing as he's had a moment to actually look at Alexis in that way realizes he finds her to be gorgeous, he keeps looking at her noting her strong legs, her shapely arms. Her profile is relaxed & calm. He looks at her short blonde hair, even after all that's happened still tied back with only a few strands of bangs loose. Alexis driving is thinking I need to check in with Uncle Jim, I can't in any way explain this over the phone but he needs to send an army if that tentacle lips thing survived. She thinks Samuel should know more, with years of experience she looks at him out of the corner of her eye, she sighs a little knowing his mind isn't on the mission she hoped he'd had time to relax & think while she talked to the highway patrol when they got pulled over, apparently he'd had a lot of time to relax....but still she thinks he's attractive enough if not a bit younger than her. She decides that needs to wait just as the last thing that was said by Jenna remembering his blushing, you just gonna ditch us for agent vagina? Knowing this isn't important now she has to ask because she doesn't remember meeting him before. Smiling a little she says, agent vagina? Samuel brought out of his fantasy clears his throat embarrassed & says well um. He explains most of it & she begins to understand. She stops him by saying, but you're dedicated now. He says I had an experience I don't want to talk about it just yet, please. She nods & says I've got a few of those. Thinking hard she asks, Samuel were you in a fire as a child? When he looks at her she knows & quickly says, sorry don't mean to pry in personal stuff but my uncle Jim, the current director in Indiana was the man that saved you, I just now remember him telling me about you. Samuel ever the southern gentleman says, your uncle the director was amazing & he will always have my appreciation for the efforts to save me & my heart still hurts for him & the people who gave their lives to save me but in the end, it wasn't just him alone. Alexis says I know Samuel in a soft voice, he looks at her wondering if she really does. Then she said nineteen other people gave their lives that day. Samuel sighs & looks away she looks at him, seeing he's thinking something says if you need to Samuel talk to me because we're in this together & I need you focused. Samuel looks at her for a moment thinking about what River & Jenna saying about trusting just Aunt Bella. He says I'll tell you when River & Jenna trust you enough Alexis because it's their family secret. She nods & says " Acceptable as long as you can focus. He says I can I'm already feeling for their location & thinking about what I should tell the director, he looks at her, and says sorry. He says honestly this is only my second mission. She looks at him & smiles nicely & says you're doing well Samuel. He smiles & nods saying nothing but thinking I should have gotten in River's car but I can at least teleport them from here. They drive in silence & when they reach the gas station he says I have to use the restroom I'll wait for you before I make any calls she nods & says I'll fill up the truck. Then she takes his arm as he goes to get out & asks Samuel it's dead, isn't it? Samuel says River doesn't think so. She nods & says we'll talk more before calling but Samuel I have killed shadows before they do not survive a 50 cal. to the head. Samuel says, & cats don't talk. As she's looking confused he says I'll be right back & goes inside. Alexis pumps gas & thinks cats don't talk? What the fuck does that mean? Regardless he believes River & until we know for certain we need to act as if it's alive. Then she thinks shit, I should have asked why the girls were headed to Portland. After a moment she realizes, he's more than attractive & I'm distracted.... damnit.

Samuel goes straight to the bathroom on the way he thinks she's connected to Bella, through her uncle yes but still is that just coincidence? Also somehow assigned to this mission. Could it be just because her uncle is in charge of the Indiana branch? That seems more likely no other reason makes sense. As he's pissing he smells an acrid stench remembering their description he knows, he shakes off staring at the wall & zips up charging for a teleport. He feels it behind him, he moves gun out safety released he spins & aims for the eyes hearing himself scream, a little happy the girls don't hear him. Click...he teleports to Alexis & says get in drive! Alexis seeing Samuel appear in front of her can't fathom what he's doing she vaguely hears it's here then she doesn't hear the rest. The Shadow Hunter appears behind him, immediately in disbelief it's alive her gun is up before she can fire it's gone, instant pain, she looks down as it raises her up thinking kill shot....that mother fucker! Then she sees Samuel right in her face & the creature roaring, it's taunting him well two can play that game & Samuel can teleport without me since I'm dead. She turns her head focusing The Shadow Hunter doesn't seem to realize what she's doing, good it's distracted, locking eyes with it she puts her gun in her left hand and raises it touching its throat she sees its eyes widen, good it knows, squeeze....the round can't miss. Then she's disoriented. When she can look up Samuel is carrying her, she smiles & thinks this will do.

River & Jenna are holding hands and talking while River drives. Excited about everything that just happened. Jenna a little shy tells River what she did to help Samuel, River smiles wide & says it's because your amazing Jenna. Jenna blushing remembers her dream & what she realized talking to Odiewan, thinking hard for a moment River notices her change & asks what's up Jenna? Jenna looks at her a long moment studying her & finally asks, are you Odiewan? River surprised at this doesn't know what to say she's shocked, finally, River says Jenna I am not a small black cat with some super crazy powers. Laughing she says ok I have some super crazy powers, but what do you mean? Jenna tells her about the dream River listens closely & tears up Jenna leans into her as she tells her dream. When she's done she says sorry River I see I was mistaken in my conclusions. River sniffles & says it's OK Jenna, I see why you thought that. She says honestly Jenna if I'm somehow Odiewan I have no clue about it. They are quite a while just before taking the offramp to Portland River says, admittedly I don't remember Odiewan before that dream & he made it sound like I should we are missing something from his riddles is all. Jenna says I agree River but it seemed so implied. River says I think that too. They stop at the gas station, & for the first time in her life, River almost forgets her hood Jenna seeing this says do it, my love. River hesitates then pulls up her hood anyway & says we can't afford attention Jenna sounding sad. Jenna takes her hand & says that may be but I'm still proud of you. They go into the gas station use the bathroom, both wash up, they get just a map & some extra food & tea. After getting gas Jenna says his address isn't far from here but should we call first? River thinks about the moment and then asks do we have time? Both thinking bout Cathululips saying no at the same time & they drive. Once there they do what they can to settle themselves & go knock on the door. It takes a lot of tries but they finally hear who is it! They look at each other hearing the anger in the man's voice. River motions at Jenna to say something & Jenna shrugs thinking what! Then says hello I'm Jenna & this is River we need to speak to Timothy Went please adding, it's important. There's silence & the two girls just stare at each other, finally, they hear, you sound young, how old are you & who sent you? River speaks & says almost seventeen & our aunt Bella sent us. Looking at Jenna shrugging as she doesn't know what else to say. After a moment they hear clicking, a lot of clicking & Jenna leans over whispering to Jenna, that's like 50 deadbolts! River stifles a laugh. The door opens a crack River has her head down holding Jenna & Jenna tries looking at him. She sees a bearded man with scraggly hair, dirty clothes & the smell they gag. Then she sees the missing right eye. The scraggly man turns his head & says look! This is what you came for, isn't it? Jenna says, I apologize for staring sir but no it's not, we didn't even know what you looked like. Eyeing the two girls he mumbles like he's talking to someone in hushed tones, what you think, not bad? Looking to see the crazy man? Oh, what's that? Yes, yes they mentioned an Aunt Bella. He looks at them seriously & asks, what's Bella's long name? The two girls are confused for a moment looking at each other then River realizing what he's asking says, Bella J. Seraph. He looks at her head turned to use his left eye, repeating Bella J. Seraph, Bella J. Seraph….yes I remember he says hushed to his invisible friend. He looks at the girl's crazy look as he says my house isn't fit for pretty young things enter at your own risk, he walks away & says lock all fify! River & Jenna just look at each other stunned about the fify. As they go in they gag & cover their mouth, there's dead what looks like half-eaten rats everywhere & garbage. Jenna pushes the door closed & looks at River questioning the logic of locking the door River looks around to make sure Timothy can't see her when she looks at Jenna again she just flashes her eyes, Jenna nods & locks the door. The two girls walk or wade through garbage, and dead rats & not wanting to see it but seeing human fecal matter & things they can't recognize. Jenna asks River in the hallway which way, River just points at the wall in front of them, Jenna looks at the wall then at River. River steps forward using her left hand and begins to light up her power lines flashing. To their amazement the wall disappears, River & Jenna just look at each other & River whispering says hell if I know!

On the other side, they walk into a clean room, looking around in amazement. They see clean chairs a table, and even a couch.

Timothy they see is sitting in front of a tv no sound watching static....he's also completely nude. River & Jenna share a look sigh & walk over. They stand a bit away watching him. Finally, River says Timothy we need to ask you about Shadow Ha...Timothy jumps from the chair running around the room, thankfully away from River & Jenna but they stand ready just in case. Finally, he stops under the table rocking himself and holding his knees to his chest. The girls seeing this realize he's traumatized & whisper to each other about what to do, finally Jenna says we have to try. River follows her holding her hand tight. When they get to the table they both kneel. He's whimpering & saying over & over again, no more, no more, no more. Jenna starts talking to him voice low & soothing, Timothy were very sorry but Aunt Bella said you could tell us of Shadow Haven &...he looks up suddenly & says & tell you I will for her! Bella nice Bella saved. He turns his head side to side squinting his eyes shut tears coming & in a little boy's voice says they won't stop! I don't wanna see the other side anymore! Then he looks up cocks his head sideways & says must hurry! He'll be baacccckkkkk! Then he says very calmly. I was born here in Portland, on 1971 October 10th. When I was five my parents died shot by the moonshine runners, they broke a moonshine bottle on my face left me to die. I was in the hospital here & after they helped me explained that I was blind in my right eye but otherwise, I had recovered. I did what I could to survive, the homes they sent me to I wasn't loved, some abused me. Finally, I was ten when they picked me up again, this time saying they were going to do something different. A woman with blonde hair blue eyes came & talked to me promising things would be better, she looked into my blind right eye holding my chin gently & said you have beautiful green & brown eyes do you know that Timothy? I believed her that everything was going to be okay & I'd see again from my right eye. Jenna & River tearing up hearing this feel for Timothy & hearing the description of the woman he spoke to they know it's Willow Fey, Jenna leans over & kisses River's cheek knowing this is going to be bad. Timothy still normal keeps talking, when I arrived the blonde woman took my hand & said follow me, Timothy, as we walked she asked what kind of soda I liked I said cola please & she smiled saying your in luck Timothy let's go get you some. I followed her to a large cafeteria, it was empty I didn't think about it then but now I know I should have. She sat me at a table & said wait here for me please, be right back. I sat there it wasn't long she came back with a can of cola & a peanut butter sandwich. I ate it all & drank the soda. As I set the can back on the table felt very tired. When I woke up I was strapped to a table, a bright light in my face. I was terrified, then Dr. Fey leaned over me from the darkness & says shhh Timothy it's OK she kissed me & said I'm going to fix that brown eye, remember I promised. I calmed a little & said ok thank you. She smiled sweetly at me & said your very welcome Timothy. Then a nurse came over & strapped my head down tight & put something on my face to force my eye open he moved away & the Dr. was back holding what I think was a spoon. She said ok Timothy I'm sorry but you have to feel this because the pain will help you see. He started getting all crazy again & his voice changed back to creepy, River & Jenna think they've lost him looking at each other tears running down their face. He yells out, THEY CUT SCOOPED

OUT MY BROWN EYE! She was right though, I could seeeee!..... EVERYTHING!! The shadows, the barriers alllll! Of it.

Outside Timothy Went's house, Samuel appears on the sidewalk holding Alexis, he looks around seeing the car, realizing they must be in the house looks down at Alexis & says you'll make it believe! Alexis too weak to do anything just lets out a moan. Timothy walks up to the door & kicks it in splitting it in half. Gagging immediately & regretting taking Alexis in steps through the doorway following the energy in his head looking for River & Jenna. He calls to them crying after a bit & keeps looking. Jenna steps out & says here Samuel from behind him when he turns around he sees a door he didn't see before. Jenna seeing Alexis says no oh no in a whisper. Samuel still hoping says she's going to make it! I need a cold bath with ice, towels, gloves & sutures now. Jenna looks at him & mouths silently at him stepping past her he walks into the room, seeing the couch he lays Alexis on it. Seeing River talking to a man he runs to them & tells the man the same thing he told Jenna. The man doesn't even look at him & keeps talking to River, saying Shadow Haven is Death Haven! Don't go there! Jenna comes up to River & takes her hand still crying turns & gestures at Alexis on the couch. River shakes her head saying it's all my fault, Jenna. Jenna grabs her looks her in the eyes & says not even a little bit! You hear me River! River sobbing nods, burying her head in Jenna's chest. After a bit Samuel grabs Timothy & shakes him saying, shut your face & talk to me! The girls & Timothy just look at Samuel confused. Timothy though looks past him sees Alexis on the couch turns his head & says rabbit hole! Turns & runs at the wall behind him, instead of hitting it he passes right through it. They just look at Alexis. River & Jenna walk over & sit beside the couch on the floor holding her hand together feeling as her life slips away remembering their grandmother. Samuel finally settles down on the armrest of the couch checking her breathing & pulse every few minutes. After an hour he says I can't believe she's still alive. Jenna says Samuel, why haven't you gone to call somebody? He jumps up, River says we would have but your the agent Samuel, sorry we didn't mention this sooner. Samuel goes to leave saying you're right I'll be as fast as I can. Then Timothy walks back in carrying a box as he approaches the girls see his left hand is gone & the bloody stump is wrapped in leaves of some sort. He looks at River who's looking up at him hood doing nothing to hide her eyes since she took it off. He looks down & smiles the calm Timothy speaking, I'm glad you don't have her eyes River. River says thank you, Timothy. Samuel looking at them confused & Jenna just keeping her mouth shut. Timothy looks at Samuel & says, she's strong Samuel & with my sacrifice will live I promise you. Samuel confused on all the levels just stands there. Timothy asks River to help, River stands up & asks what do I do Timothy? He says just hold my box only I can touch what's inside because it's my gift. She holds the box & he opens it. Reaching inside he pulls out his left hand still very much alive & moving. Samuel says fuck that! Pointing his gun at Timothy, Timothy just looks at him waiting, River says Samuel, Samuel look at me. He does & River says think about it she's almost dead & will die probably before you can go & bring help here. Jenna quietly says Samuel, when he looks at her she's got tears in her eyes not knowing if Alexis will make it or not & she whispers down boy listen to River. Samuel tearing up looks at Timothy & nods putting his gun away. Timothy says thank you, & lays his squirming severed hand on her head. Nothing seems to happen then the hand falls on the floor dead leaking blood. Timothy picks it up & walks over to the door & opens it throwing it out with the other garbage he comes back & says she'll be fine in a day or so. He points at the door on the far side of the room & says toiletries & kitchen. He looks at all of them one by one tears in his eyes & says, worth it! Falling over dead.

Chapter 16

Nullsoul searches for his prey's scent finding it he follows. When he finds the end of the trail he sees a structure that confuses him. He circles it twice, but can't sense inside. It's growing dark & he's thinking about testing the structure because in his fazed state he should be able to pass through it. Then the pain comes he collapses curling up & screaming if possible it's worse than ever. He hears The Unseen One's voice. You still fail Nullsoul, we will tolerate this no more! He thinks to himself they are going to kill me....so be it he knows if he's dead nothing will matter. Probably hearing his thoughts they speak again. You will never leave that realm with our help again, you are marked & banished, if you are found outside that realm you will be brought to us & tortured until even we cannot restore you. If you are as brave & skilled hunter as you believe continue the pursuit of your prey your hatred can have you & then nothing no pain & no voices. Nullsoul stands, I have been permanently banished....again tortured for something, not of my own doing. All I have now is her death....he remembers something it flooding in. He escaped from the place the human, that's what they are! The place the human had held him. He remembers he'd finally grown strong enough to break his chains, after that the cell door was easy. He had followed their scents hunting all of them. He searched for her scent the most and he'd found her as well. As he was feeding on the last human she was fleeing with a small one in her arms. Something he didn't know what made her turn around beside one of the small moving structures, looking right at him. She said something to the small one in her arms & it turned & looked at him.....the eyes! Large jade green eyes looked at him from the small one! The Shadow Girl, the prey! They came from the same place. Then he looked into the moving structure from where he stood enjoying the feeding still, that small black cat watching him amused look on its face in the back of the moving structure. Searching his memories more the small black cat had mentioned he don't remember it but why? Not from that singular moment for sure. Then he remembers, for a time the cat visited in the cell & it used to talk to him. He remembers! It used her voice then too. They talked a lot but last they spoke the cat had asked him, if you leave this place what will you do? Nullsoul not Nullsoul then, but he had answered, I want to kill them all. The black cat asked them all. He replied simply all that is not me. The small black cat looked sad & said, one day Shadow Hunter we will meet at low noon & shadows will fall. After a short pause, the cat said still looking him in the eyes, till then this is goodbye. He never seen it again until the night of the first hunt of The Shadow Girl. Why does it protect her? Before he thinks about it more he decides to act, moving towards the structure and deciding to enter it. Then walking from behind the front step The Small Black Cat stops in front of the structure & looks up at him sitting an amused look on its face. Still, with the prey's voice, it says welcome Shadow Hunter low noon approaches. Nullsoul stops not fleeing but thinks of this & realizes the time in this realm, it's close to halfway before its sun shines. Nullsoul looks at the cat & says I remember you now. The cat says, have you changed your perspective since then Nullsoul? Nullsoul thinking why would he know me by that name? However since he's proud he decides to answer, no I have not I will even kill you. The small black cat lowers its head sounding sad and says if you wish to try Shadow Hunter you may begin. Nullsoul thinks for just a moment & says I will only kill you after I have killed The Shadow Girl I want you to see her end. Then Nullsoul says you choose her over me. The cat still looking sad says no Nullsoul you chose her over yourself. Nullsoul confused growls at the cat, then says explain! The cat is quiet a moment then says. When you stopped loving anything but ending life you chose her over yourself. You had a choice. Nullsoul about to contradict the cat sees another memory, one from the golden-haired woman that kept him chained. She asked Nullsoul if he loves her because he never said it & she did tell him she loved him. His reply was if this is love I want to never know it. After the memory, the cat says now you see, because of that River was born. Nullsoul rages & attempts to hurt the cat but it's gone, no scent & no energy. Nullsoul just says aloud your time will come cat. He tries entering the structure but fails fazed he can't pass through it, unfazed he can't damage it, so he decides to wait.

River & Jenna move Timothy outside the room where he'd thrown his severed hand not sure what else to do. Jenna & River standing there in the muck Jenna asks, should we say anything? River says aloud, find your peice Timothy you have earned it. They stand there in silence for a moment then return to the room with Samuel & Alexis. He's on the floor beside her head down holding her hand. River whispering to Jenna says let's go see the toiletries & kitchen. They walk past them Samuel doesn't raise his head. Inside the other room, they are happy with what they find. A full kitchen is well stocked & the food isn't out of date. The bathroom has a big tub designed for sitting, Jenna says to River we will be using that very soon, River says yes love. Then they see the clean bed both urging to use it. They cook first. They make a big meal. Steak potatoes, asparagus, & cheese-covered pasta. Before they eat they get a serving tray & put enough on it for Samuel & Alexis in case she wakes up. Of course with servings of black tea. River grabs a butter bowl & places a stick-o-butter in it seeing this she looks at River, River says it may cheer him up knowing we're thinking of him, Jenna just softly smiles. Jenna carrying the food tray walks it out to them Samuel's head is still down. They place it next to him & get back to their meal. After cuddling in a hot tub River says Jenna I'm thinking that after you & I sleep we go to Shadow Haven by ourselves. Jenna looks at her curled in her arms & says why River? River says, I don't want them hurt by Cathululips & he can't reach them here. Jenna says, not that I don't believe you River but how do you know? River says I don't know how I know it but we are not in our place. Jenna asks, place? River thinks about it a moment & says closest I have to explaining it is our dimension. They are quiet for a little bit & then Jenna kisses River's neck & says ok River we can leave them. River running her fingertips slowly along Jenna's abdomen asks her are you sure? Jenna says yes, they have both suffered enough for us. River looks at her & says, from now until forever sweet Jenna & kisses her. They sleep in the tub.

The girls wake up a few hours later the water in the tub to cold to sleep in anymore. Jenna giggling & having fun with River about their wrinkly skin. They grab a quick bite to eat & quietly peek out the door to the other room still sitting there head down is Samuel holding Alex's hand. River & Jenna look at each other & decide to go. As they walk by trying to be extra quiet they notice Samuel ate. Jenna looks at the butter bowl its open & she grabs her mouth giggling. River smiles & looks at Alexis sleeping. But she's not asleep. Looking at her a moment River waves at her & Alexis gives her a sad smile. After the girls get out of the room Jenna asks, do you think she knows River silently nods yes. Jenna says I hope she doesn't tell Samuel. They walk outside it's predawn & they look around, Jenna sniffs the air then looks at River, River says, I don't feel it. Jenna sighs in relief & says let's go before anything can change its mind.

Samuel woke up sometime later having to use the toilet he checks Alexis first & her eyes opened as he's listening to her breathing. She knows what he's doing & smiles & whispers in his ear good morning my knight. He turns his head surprised then he starts to lean back but she raises her left hand placing it on his shoulder & says against his face, you don't have to move Samuel. He blushes & says, I'm afraid I have to for at least a moment I really need to pee. Alexis starts giggling then gives him a gentle kiss & says hurry back. Samuel shocked not sure what to do nods & goes to the bathroom trying to not disturb the girls if they are sleeping. When he goes in the kitchen he sees it's cleaned up looking towards the bed nervously in the back he doesn't see them he walks up to it. He thinks a minute it's made. He walks to the bathroom gently knocking on the door, with no response & no noise from inside he opens the door enough to see in, no one? He goes inside the air is still damp & smells of wet bodies. Looking in the tub he sees some black & blonde hair in the drain screen. They left! He pees & runs back to Alexis.

Alexis lays there & smiles to herself, thinking that was a pretty ok kiss. Laughing at herself she decides to sit up, it goes ok, looking around she sees the food on the tray reaching out she feels a little pain but pushes through setting the plate in her lap, taking a deep breath stomach growing like she hadn't eaten in a month she digs in. Samuel comes out looking flustered. Alexis looks up at him & smiles as he walks over, seeing the look on his face she knows he's realized the girls are gone, swallowing her bite of steak she says Samuel when he looks at her she just taps the couch with her left hand. He moves around & sits down. Immediately he says I can't find River & Jenna. Alexis nodding mouth full of food holds her hand up signaling for him to wait. After she eats she wipes her hands & mouth then drinks some tea seeing Samuel being impatient, she thinks to herself smiling, bless his big heart. Then she turns to him taking his hands & says they left a while ago Samuel. He asks when, she looks around smirk on her face & says where's the clock? He gets it & nods saying ok. She says Samuel, I need to use the toilet make sure I make it, please. He immediately puts his right arm around her & when she's ready they stand up with a big sigh she says ok not so bad ready? Samuel says yes & they walk to the toilet. Alexis is happy it was under her own power. Sitting there peeing she talks to his back. I think I can go with you Samuel but first, we need to call and get ALOT of backup. He says where am I going? Standing pulling up her pants she says after River & Jenna. He turns his head in time to see a flash of blonde hair, turns immediately back around & says I um...she giggles at him then flushes & says I know you're going because I am too. He turns around & she's standing there looking at him seriously. Samuel trying to pick his battles & realizing he losing says ok, ok we'll go. She takes his hand & decides to tease him as they are walking out, did you get to see anything you liked? His blushing says all she needs to know.

Nullsoul watches as the Shadow Girl & its mate leave the structure through the broken entrance they are alone. He sees though they are ready & he thinks carefully about his next move. Watching them they get in their small mobile structure, he decides to follow & wait for his chance.

Sometime during low noon...The small black cat is sitting on Alexis's chest looking at her as usual an amused look on his face waiting. As her eyes flutter open & she takes a big breath she looks around immediately feeling the small pressure on her chest. She looks at the cat a moment & in a weak voice says, well...hello you are you comfortable? Hearing River's voice in her head, yes thank you, Alexis, I know you are not but you will be soon, Timothy's gift was strong & with your own strength, you'll do well. She just looks at him a moment & through her fatigued brain remembers Samuel saying, "& cats don't talk". She smiles at the cat & it he nuzzles her chin with its head purring slightly. When its done it leans back sitting contently. Alexis looks at it a moment & then asks, do Samuel & I follow River & Jenna? The cat is quite a moment & then says, you & Samuel must write your own stories, futures not set, fates not decided. Then the cat says, however, Alexis you ask questions to things you already know the answer to. Alexis smiles weakly & says yes kitty but sometimes it helps to do so & hear the other's answers. The cat says it does...Alexis you know what you have to do I'm just here to meet & support a new friend. She smiles & asks what is your name kitty? It looks at her amused & says you just told me. Alexis musters enough strength to pet him & asks, what do you think of my knight? Eyes looking at Samuel. The cat just says you've chosen well. Alexis exhausted returns to sleep smiling.

Chapter 17

River & Jenna follow the map as carefully as they can, some thirty miles outside Portland, the dirt road they are on seems to have not been traveled in some time. River driving looking around a little tense she finally says I know this place, Jenna. Jenna looks around too seeing the forest she recognizes having grown up in Oregon says you take me to the nicest places love. River looks at her just a moment then busts out laughing, they both have a good laugh.

Nullsoul follows his prey, he knows this place they are returning to the beginning.....fitting he thinks, you will die where you began.

Samuel & Alexis get to a phone she tells Samuel you call I'll take inventory, Samuel surprised asks shouldn't you? She looks at him a moment & says, you know the situation & you know what we need & who needs us. Then she steps close seeing Samuel is still nervous of her asks, why are you nervous with me Samuel? Flustered & not sure how to say it he just blurts out....YOU'RE MY FIRST! Alexis smiles softly & says I understand Samuel, do you want me to take this slower? Samuel thinks a moment then says, I have no correct answers… I'll try to keep up with you Alexis. She smiles then kisses him softly & says I'll be gentle, now go call, please. Samuel calls & when he does no one picks up, he tries twice to no avail returning to the suburban he sees Alexis in body armor, she sees him handing him a chest plate & says it might be better than nothing. He takes off his coat & as he's putting it on he says we're dark…that's the correct term for when they don't answer right? She hesitates taking in what he said & then says yes. Then he says I believe we have to decide which takes precedence then. He looks at her worries shell say they have to go to Indiana now. Samuel sees her looking at him then her eyes wonder, they are at a small gas station outside Portland the road to Shadow Haven not far, sitting on a fence post The Small Black Cat watches them watching him. Samuel looks at her before he can speak she says Kitty with a smile & Samuel says see?! Cats talking? She chuckles & says Samuel, sweety you're my knight, and I'm going for the girls I already know what your big heart has decided. Samuel smiles at her & says, I told the director if we lose them we lose everything, I think now I know what I meant. Putting her hand on his shoulder & stepping to the ground she looks at him & says, I do too. As they drive away the black cat watches from the fence post still content.

Nullsoul follows his prey trying to remain patient, they are taking far too long he thinks maybe it's fear. As he follows them he feels they are close & he also feels other's close, moving towards the new energies he sees cloth structures rocks stacked in a circle & a fire in it. The humans are a mixed group of males & females. He doesn't understand all that they are doing but he believes they are enjoying themselves. He feels their minds & is excited, all but two of them will be useful if he needs to feed. He knows he'll need to be wise because he knows that if he feeds on one the others will flee.

It took River & Jenna around an hour to navigate the dirt road but finally coming around the last corner they see a three-story building with a four-car garage to its right, River stops & looks at the dirt purposefully piled in the road. The girls talk for a moment grabbing bags & filling them with food, water & some tea, then taking each other's hand & a deep breath go to the building. As they approach River stops in the driveway as Jenna looks at her she sees something happening, Jenna asks if she's OK & River just nods, Jenna looks around nervous & waits for whatever River is going through. River remembers, her mother carrying her & seeming nervous, in her little young voice, River asks where are we going, Mom? Her mother just said away & try to be quiet, please. River hears screaming & loud noises as they hurry through the building outside, once outside her mother picked her up & ran. Once she stopped running she whispered in River's ear, say goodbye to your brother & turned around & said there, & Young River looked & saw a shadowy figure standing a ways away swaying slightly from side to side looking back at them. River angry, says no! Not...My...Fucking...Brother! Jenna hears her & looks at her worried, River turns to her sighs rolling her eyes, and quietly says I remember my mother carrying me from here....she um...said say goodbye to your brother standing her by a car. River bites her lip hoping Jenna understands. Jenna thinking hard seeing River isn't saying something thinks she understands & says I don't see any resemblance. River tears up letting out the breath she was holding & says quietly, thank you, Jenna. Jenna hugs her holding her tight.

Nullsoul watches them seeing what's happening to The Shadow Girl he's joyed. She remembers! & it causes her pain....good!

Driving down the dirt road they see the fresh tire tracks & Alexis says we're on the right track. Samuel says we better be unless there are two Shadow Havens, Alexis says I certainly hope not. Then she asks Samuel I just thought about this myself but did you call both numbers? Samuel said yes & both were no response. Alexis is really nervous now, for H.Q. not to answer that's one thing but the emergency number is even in Indiana, she doesn't know where it is but knows nobody does for that reason. They drive on coming up behind River's car after she looks around for a moment she takes Samuel's hand & says, Samuel make sure we live through this. Samuel says I will Alexis & that goes for all four of us. After they get their gear set up they share an awkward hug through body armor & a kiss, then they soldier up looking for River & Jenna.

River & Jenna were surprised the front door was open, after nervous glances at each other they went in. They entered a large square room, the wallpaper was peeling at the corners, broken furniture strewn about with some broken glass & brown stains on

River's Shadow

the floors & walks. In the back was a staircase, looking up there River said, my room is up there. Before Jenna can ask if she wants to go take a look, they hear a thud & a door sliding across the floor. Looking in that direction they see a figure approaching, wearing an old raggy lab coat & scraggly blonde hair, mumbling something about not being able to find my socks. River & Jenna just look at each other not even being surprised anymore. When they see it getting closer they realize it's a woman. Suddenly she stops & looks up at them, not saying anything but River recognizes her & in a flat voice says, it lives still Jenna. Jenna putting it together & seeing the one picture of River's mother, sighs & says in a half-hearted tone, I always wanted to meet your mother. River does chuckle a little but just keeps her eyes locked on her mother. Willow starts laughing & finally stopping says, come to dig up the family skeletons have you, daughter? Before River can reply Willow spins around head back arms out laughing historically, then stopping and rushes up to River, River's eyes glow & her skin starts to light up. Willow chuckles & says oohhh don't be scared of Mommy mommy loves you. River says flat out not here for that never got it before don't expect it now. Willow acts hurt saying oh don't be like that to Mommy, all I did ever did was give you the best a loving mother could give her darling daughter. River glares at her but contains her anger & says, I just want some answers, please. Willow wooppss & carries on a minute & says, first a question, where's my darling sister? Or did she forsake you as well? River hides the sadness not believing her mother deserves to see it & says Aunt Bella has passed. Willow looks at her for a moment confusion, shock, & maybe even sadness across her face, then she chuckles & says my sweet River, your answers are here look around, then Willow lowers her head looking at her & in a low voice says, but you & your blonde slut stay out of the basement it's mine. Then she turns to her left laughing skips across the room to the far door & yells back as she's holding the door & says welcome home! Jenna not sure what to think or do just stood there watching holding River's hand. Sighs & says we'll, she's a bag of crazy dicks. River looks at her with a serious look on her face. Jenna worried she offended River starts to apologize, but River smiles softly & says, uncircumcised to be sure. They share a giggle then River looks back upstairs & sighs. Jenna says when your ready my love.

Nullsoul watches as the prey talks to the creator as he will never call it mother. He listens & watches them engage with one another, noting his prey's body language he sees both of them have changed more confident, more alert. He also notes The Shadow Girl's immediate defense to possible danger, knowing she will be a challenging fight. He thinks after he will kill the creator & leave her corpse in a place the prey will find it. After the engagement ends he watches, it takes them some time to decide where to go it seems, they chose to go higher in the structure. He's set to follow when he hears something outside. He thinks it must be the other two prey, he moves outside & sees he's correct. Contemplating he decides to eliminate them now, the four of them together is too great a risk. As they approach the entrance he decides to take them in the open, believing he is faster & being able to teleport has the advantage. He eyes the female a moment not sure why she isn't dead or why she moves without pain. Then decides it doesn't matter, he'll take the head this time.

As Samuel & Alexis approach the entrance Alexis gets that sense again…being hunted! She immediately crouches & signals Samuel, two fingers pointing at her eyes & motioning at both of them. Samuel understands & looks around crouched as well. Then tentacle lips appears between them he swipes at Alexis's head first thinking she the worst threat, she moves getting clawed down the back of her body armor, taking some flesh as well. Samuel seeing this with little time to react takes a big chance, he thinks shooting Cathululips is pointless & even if they hurt it enough it will just teleport & hide until it's recovered. So with an inhuman speed, he drops the rifle he was carrying before it can even hang from the sling his hands grab a block of c4 from the pouch on his side, grabs his knife & rams it through the c4 arms its electronic fuse & rams the blade deep into Cathululips's lower back, then braces. Nullsoul feeling a twinge in his lower back knows the other prey did something & seeing the female prey avoided his death blow, spins to attack the male. Claw ready he makes contact burying them deep into the male, it lets out its scream. Nullsoul in contact with the prey's body feels it try to teleport but Nullsoul absorbs the energy keeping its prey held. Alexis rolling from the claw comes up ready gun pointed at tentacle lips. Then she sees what Samuel has done, the block of c4 stuck to its lower back. She thinks to herself smart Samuel very smart. Then seeing he's pinned realizes he can't teleport besides they are much too close if they hope to survive detonating the c4. She moves quickly tucks the combat shotgun she decided to carry under the armpit connected to the claw buried in Samuel's upper arm...lightening fast ten rounds fire as as fast as the shotguns firing pin can pierce the back of the buckshot rounds she'd loaded. She smiles as she sees it works, it doesn't take his arm off but it makes him swing with it at her, ducking she sees Samuel thrown free, then runs hoping Samuel can & is ready to detonate. As Alexis is diving into the front door of the building she hears the explosion & everything shakes & dust from the building covers her body.

Nullsoul retreats to the prey that he'd selected before the hunter feeding on all of them hes able. Infuriated that the weaker of the prey did this to him making him use up his food source, he didn't even kill them! Thinking about his options he decides to move quickly he'll just have to kill the Shadow Girl & her mate the source of his hatred. If he's strong enough when it's over he will kill the other two, they should be weaker now improving his chances

Standing outside a closed door River & Jenna hold hands both nervous. River staring at the door says, Jenna, I really need you to say something funny & sarcastic right now. Jenna knows River is leaning on her for strength and tries to think of something.... she says we'll um I've been thinking & I...well, she sighs River is looking at her now. Jenna looks at her shyly & asks can our honeymoon be on a private yacht somewhere in the Caribbean? Jenna looking nervous, shy, & extremely awkward fidgets while she waits for River's answer to her proposal. River's mouth moves making no sound mouth turned up in a huge grin and finally asks Jenna did you just...you want...then says, Yes oh very much fucking yes! Jenna tearing up says I um have been waiting for the right moment to talk to you bout this but um ya sooo...we're getting married? River puts her face to Jenna's & says yes I do believe we are wife! They kiss, and as they kiss they hear gunshots & River looks in Jenna's eyes and says we better hurry! They turn & River opens her childhood bedroom door. As they walk in they look around, kids drawings on the walls & toys in a toy box in one corner next to a bed, on the bed is a cardboard box. Jenna looking around at the drawings sees one of Cathululips or at least she thinks it is, deciding it's better to move past that without comment she stops at the drawing of a black cat under it something is written, looking closer she sees it's not just the bad handwriting of a child it's just not a language she recognizes. River looking around and seeing the cardboard box on the bed thinks that's what Mom....Willow meant by answers I need to see what's in it. Looking at Jenna saying Hey she sees Jenna just staring at the wall, she tries to get her attention but can't. Then the whole building shakes from an explosion & River reacting as fast as she can has herself & Jenna under the bed. After a moment she hears Jenna beside her ask, River...are we under a bed? River turns her head to look at her & laughs & says yes love we are. Jenna confused just says we'll weve done it all now. Laughing as they get out from under the bed, River asks Jenna if she's ok. Jenna says I'm fine but something did happen to me before I found myself under the bed next to you. Then she sighs a little nervous & shows River the cat & writing. Jenna says do you know what it says River? River looks at it a moment then says no but I feel I should. Looking at Jenna she asks, do you? Jenna looking awkward says we'll um....Odiewan. River looks at her eyebrows raised & says amazing Jenna. Jenna smiles & says I don't know, but I know. River says I believe you. River grabs her hand & takes her to the box on the bed. They open it there are three binders in it. The first one on top says Journal Of Willow Fey, & below that the second says the River Experiment. River & Jenna just look at each other for a moment then both look in the box at the last journal. Shadow Hunter Experiment, under that the word "success?" The girls grab the journal & put all three in their bags. River says should we go to the basement? Jenna says we'll the crazy bag of uncircumcised dicks says no but....& River laughs saying we don't remember hearing that right? They laugh heading downstairs to look for the basement stairs. At the entrance they see Samuel & Alexis patching each other up. The girls look at each other smiling & walk toward them. Then River feels Cathululips, and before she can say anything he's above both of them she sees just a small flicker then she & Jenna are crashing through the floor. She hears Jenna scream & sees Cathululips hit her hard, River lights up turning ready to land on her feet & finish him.

Holding River's hand Jenna is excited to see Samuel & Alexis, & she knows they can help her & River....then suddenly she realizes she's falling looking up she sees Cathululips & then he hits her hitting the floor all she can do is moan he stands over her she can barely see, but she smiles seeing River's glow standing up behind him as she blacks out her last thought was of River....from now till always...

River standing on her feet sees Cathululips standing over Jenna she looks at Jenna thinking good bye my sweet love. Then she attacks hitting him so hard she drives him into the stone wall & she immediately follows he vanishes expecting him to come from behind she turns & nothing is there except Jenna's corpse. Then pain, she feels him behind & he's driven both claws through her small torso from behind. She sees the shadows cast by her glow & calls to them, growing bigger & darker as they come. River directs them to attack Cathululips & they move followed by his roar, she's thrown against the far wall. River hearing his pain rolls over to watch not sure what the shadows are doing to him but she can see they are passing through him & each time he roars. As Cathululips falls to one knee he looks directly at her & says we both die this day sister. She hears the menace & hatred in his voice, then he moves, standing over her raining blows down on her & she feels it, looking at Jenna she tears up & thinks…till death do we part my love.

As Jenna falls unconscious she hears her grandmother's voice. She's back four months ago In her grandmother's home & grandma's alive! Jenna runs to her hugging crying telling her how much she missed her & loves her. Her grandmother holds her & lets her cry & soothes her. When she's done her grandmother says look at me, Jenna. Jenna looks up hugging her still. Her grandmother says, I love you too & I miss you every second but I am also not sorry. I lived my life all four hundred & fifty years of it & I lived long enough to have you in it & see you find your calling, your one. Jenna listening is confused about her grandmother's age but also…

my calling?....my one? Then her grandmother says Jenna listen & she does. Death will do that to you, & my being here isn't helping so I'll try to help you. Her grandmother just says one word, River. Suddenly it all floods back in & Jenna remembers everything & she remembers dying. She cries again. Her grandmother asks her, do you love your River? Do you love your wife? Jenna says, until forever. Her grandmother smiles brightly. Then her grandmother takes a step back & starts glowing, after a moment Jenna sees her grandmother young, tall & strong. Then from behind her, she hears Im so proud of you Jenna. Jenna turns in shock her aunt Bella standing there. Jenna runs & hugs her. Bella smiling says I love you too Jenna. Then leaning back she puts her hands on her shoulders & looks Jenna in the eye. She says Jenna, you have a choice to make. You can die happy & content with the life you lived or you can go back & live many, many years beside River. It's your choice & only you can decide which one is the right one. Jenna sniffles a little thinking & looks back at her grandmother still standing there a soft smile on her young face. Jenna thinking finally looks at Bella & says, this is not the until forever River & I promised to each other. Bella smiles & says go be her sword, then feeling her grandmother's hands on her back hears her say, go be her shield.

Jenna wakes up looking around seeing Cathululips pounding her sweet River to death & without hesitating is on her feet. Feeling a sword materialize in her right hand she moves sliding under Cathululips between his legs strikes out cutting the right leg off. Jenna is immediately on her feet as he lashes out her left hand comes up & on her forearm is a triangle of light. She leans into it taking his blow & immediately swings her sword taking his arm. Kneeling in front of her on one bloody stump of a severed leg he looks her in the eyes. Without hesitation, Jenna takes his head. When she sees he's dead & the shadows in the room dissipate she turns to River sword & shield disappearing. Jenna kneels beside River taking her into her lap pulling her head close knowing she'll want to be against her breast. Jenna remembering what happened while she was dead tears up thinking if I came back just to mourn my love....she can't continue, sobbing overtaking her. Jenna doesn't know how long she sobbed holding River but when she felt River's right arm embrace her she had no words for the joy & love that filled her heart. Looking into River's eyes crying, River looked at her & said wife, I need a vacation. They laughed for a while then Jenna asked, your ok right? River says I am don't know why but I'm fine Jenna. Then River looks at her & you Jenna? I saw you die. Jenna sniffles & says I did, but it's ok I saw grandma & aunt Bella they are very happy for us & very proud! River tears up.

Samuel & Alexis heard the crashing behind them & Jenna's scream. They both jumped up & ran to the edge of the hole in the floor. Seeing The Shadow Hunter & then River lighting up. Samuel immediately said we have to get down there! He even tries stepping off. Alexis grabs him pulling him back. She says stop, think! We can't just jump down there into the dark we can't help them with both our legs shoved up our asses. Samuel nods & says ok we do it another way. Alexis looks around Seeing the Small Black Cat at the doorway looking expectant at them & she smiles pulling Samuel behind her this way hurry. As they are running he asks where we going? All Alexis says is kitty. She follows the cat around the side of the building. It pacing next to a cellar door in the ground. She runs up saying thank you kitty. Samuel looks at the cat & chuckles pulling on the door Alexis grunts then says stop laughing you and help. He does they get the heavy door open looking down into darkness. Alexis starts to step forward & Samuel grabs her stopping her & steps in front of her cracking a green glowstick. She smiles at his back & scratches kitties head with her fingers as she follows her knight into the darkness.

River & Jenna finally stand up from the stone floor & look around holding each other's hand. Jenna asks, can you see anything River? River's eyes glowing says yes....surprisingly. Jenna says ya me too. They start walking down the tunnel. River asks, remember the books we read about exploring catacombs? Jenna says ya, voice shaking a little. River asks is it too late to change my mind about trying it? That makes Jenna chuckle & she says we both can right now. As they walk through the darkness they only smell dust & see an empty tunnel. It's not very long before they see a glow ahead. They both stop heads pressed together. Jenna says I feel something River. River says me too Jenna my body is vibrating & I hear a pulse in the air. Jenna says we can look for another way. River asks her if she seen one & Jenna says no damnit. River says ya me neither. Sighing they start walking again, stepping around the corner they see what's putting off the light. In the center of the room is a large sphere about five feet in diameter hovering above the floor. The sphere appears to be black liquid somehow contained in the shape of a sphere. Jenna asks River if she knows what it is & when River doesn't answer Jenna looks at her & takes a step back. River's large jade green eyes aren't jade green anymore, to Jenna's fears they are black voids just like Cathululips. Jenna cries out to River trying to get her attention but River only responds by slowly taking a step towards the sphere. Jenna moves fast stepping between River & the sphere. River looks at Jenna & cocks her head to the side. Finally, all Jenna can think to do is say River you're hurting me! It works River steps back shaking her head closing her eyes she turns sideways away from the sphere. Quietly River says Jenna? Jenna says yes River. River's eyes still closed says if you want to keep me & keep this realm safe take my hand & guide me away from here now! Jenna scared listens she takes River's hand seeing her eyes are closed & says this way love. Jenna confused & worried wonders what's happening but keeps guiding River down the tunnel. Suddenly River stops tugging on Jenna's hand. Jenna looks back & River has her head turned to the side like she's listening to something. Quietly Jenna says, River? River turns her head suddenly eyes open & to Jenna's relief, Jade Green says run!

Alexis follows Samuel into the dark, following a tunnel. Several minutes pass & Samuel says shit! Looking over his shoulder Alexis sees a big thick steel door. Looking at it she sees it's recessed in concrete & there's no handle. There's maybe a keyhole but it's not like one she's seen before. It's just an oval indentation, Samuel looks at her saying explosives? Hope in his voice. Alexis sighs & says the explosives necessary to blow that door will level the entire house burying it. Samuel nods he already suspected this. Then from the dark in the tunnel behind them, they hear a voice, a female voice saying, some Watchers of Shadow you two are. They spin around guns drawn. They hear a laugh & then silence. Focusing on the dark they hear something that sounds like a glass marble hitting the concrete & roll to them stopping as it bumps into Alex's combat boot. After a moment & there's nothing but silence Alexis cautiously picks up a solid black marble, she sees it's big enough for the indentation in the door. She looks at Samuel & says try it? A question in her tone. He takes it & says we have nothing else to try. He turns & puts it in the indentation & they hear locks clicking & rods sliding against stone. They look at each other & shrug. They turn to look down the tunnel & before they take a step they hear the sound of tennis shoes on stone running. Getting ready pointing their guns into the tunnel they see two white orbs moving side to side just ahead of it to the right of it two jade green ones. Alexis calls out, Jenna! River! This way! They hear River, stone cold calm....run!

As they run River pulls ahead but doesn't let go of Jenna's hand. Jenna asks what is it? River sounding calm & distant says it's the other side & they are commanding me to open the gateway between realms. Jenna asks realms. River replies, dimensions. Jenna says well, shit. River says exactly. They run & as they are coming around the corner they see Samuel & Alexis in the distance & to both girl's relief behind them their eyes can pick up the starlight. When they hear Alexis call to them River gives one response...run! Thankfully they listened & turned & ran. Getting to the door River rushes Jenna through it. Jenna immediately thinks River is leaving her side, River!? River just grabs the door pulling it closed then extends her right hand, Jenna watches as the orb shoots out from the door into River's palm. River turns to her & says this orb is the key to the door, love. River looks at her, then says I'm the key to the portals. Jenna looks at her understanding. River says, as long as I have until forever my sweet Jenna I won't allow them through. Then the orb recedes into River's palm. Jenna sniffles & says as long as I have until forever I'll be by your side. They hold each other kissing. They head out Alexis & Samuel waiting. When Alexis asked what happened River said its what Aunt Bella told us, this place was Shadow Haven a Watchers of Shadow guarded a portal here. Samuel asks then why were you girls panicking? They look at each other & do their best to blush. Jenna looks up at them shyly & says it's very dark down there. Alexis & Samuel seem to buy it & hug the girls saying they are safe now. As the sun rises they are eating breakfast at the vehicles. Jenna & River giggling at each other bring an object to Samuel & Alexis who are also eating & sitting very close together. When they approach they are all teenage girl. Giggling & whispering. Alexis looks at them & smiles & asks what are you two up to? The girls look at each other conspiring & Jenna says well now that you two are an item we wanted to give you something. Of course, Samuel blushes & Alexis smiles & says you girls are so sweet. Then River holds up her hand an object in it wrapped in a cloth napkin. She looks at Samuel & says you should do it, Samuel. Smiling & blushing he humbly accepts the gift, asking when do we open it? The girls can't help but giggle, Alexis watching as she has an idea they are just teasing Samuel again. Finally, Jenna says oh whenever you feel the need. Then River says hug us you two were going home. They hug them & say goodbyes. Then River says you two need to tell your people something for us please & anyone else that needs to hear it. Seeing River's serious hearing her tone they listen. She says, leave us alone & do not come looking for us. Then she says Alexis Anora, and Samuel Nigeus, you two are welcome to visit anytime. Alexis & Samuel smile & Alexis says well deliver your message & warn them as well if need be enforce it. The girls say thank you. As the girls get to their car & head for home in the backseat a Small Black Cat is curled up sleeping on Jenna's hoodie.

After the girls leave Alexis says open our gift, Samuel. Samuel blushes & hesitates & Alexis asks what's wrong? He says I have a feeling this is a practical joke. Then adds with love though. Alexis smiles & says do you want me to open holding out her hand. He considers it and then hands it to her, she opens the cloth napkin inside is a stick-o-butter. Seeing this taking the joke very well Samuel laughs. When he's done Alexis says explain. He blushes & hides his face. Alexis says well I think you know the way to the highway. He looks at her & she's loaded up getting into the driver's seat of the suburban. He goes to the passenger side she has the door locked & acting like she's considering something cracks the window & doesn't look at him but asks, you ready to tell? He explains the joke she's already laughing when he says "I love the smell of tuna & eggs in the morning" She unlocks the door & says I love you Samuel now get in. Smiling he puts his left hand on the seat to climb in something brushes his hand. He sees a white piece of plastic in the fold of the seat, pulling it out he immediately feels what it is. Turning it over he confirms it's the picture of Bella....he feels her presence.

About the Author

Timothy Went, a vibrant author, was born forty-two years ago on the southern border of the United States. His life's journey inspired him to channel his imagination onto paper, creating captivating stories. The result is his latest work, Rivers Shadow, a testament to his creativity and passion for storytelling. Timothy's writing journey is driven by the pleasure he derives from it and his desire to share this joy with his readers. His works are designed to appeal to anyone aged 16 and above who relishes a good tale. We hope you enjoy reading his work as much as he enjoyed writing it.

www.ingramcontent.com/pod-product-compliance
Lightning Source LLC
LaVergne TN
LVHW051950060526
838201LV00059B/3588